ISBN 1-894372-04-2

Overtime

D. Brad Janes

Thanks for reading

Hope you enjoy!

A special thank you goes to my wife and at-home editor Shelley Janes for her critical eye; my daughters Kailey and Kenzie, may you both enjoy the love of the written word; my father and mother Doug and Alexis for never standing in front of me, but always standing behind me; my sister Gina' for unending support; Ivy Cosman for introducing me to the literary world all those years ago; Doug and Andrea Ackerley for encouragement; Steve Vair for believing; David Henley and Deanna Bradley for my start; Mike Carter for fiddling; the Janes' boys back home. Finally to Monica Hughes for first reading; Yvonne Wilson and Elizabeth Margaris for taking me in off the street and showing me the ropes. Your energy levels are amazing. Thanks somehow doesn't seem enough to all of you.

Brad Janes, fall, 1999

FOREWORD

I got to know Brad Janes during the fall of 1994 when we were both starting out. Myself as a goaltender with the Calgary Flames minor hockey league affiliate and Brad as the beat writer for the Saint John Flames. Over the years we got to know each other and somehow forged a friendship that skirted the boundaries of myself being a player and Brad being a sportswriter.

I recall a bus trip from Syracuse to Montreal when we spoke for hours. My ambition back then was to become a goaltender in the National Hockey League and Brad someday wanted to become a published writer.

We've both reached our goals.

As a writer Brad is accurate and at times brutally honest. Generally, players don't have a problem with that as long as its consistent and I believe that's what Brad is as he writes for the Flames.

In 'Overtime' the description of the players and the atmosphere is unbelievably real. Brad takes his readers on the ride through an 80 game season and lets them know how tough it is even at the best of times. He takes his readers through the dressing room, training camp and the trials of being a professional hockey player. You get a feel for the inner workings of a newsroom and the front office of a minor professional hockey team.

I'm an avid reader and always searching for a book to keep my interest. My hockey connection to 'Overtime' caught interest as, after having played in the minors for 2 years before getting to Calgary and Buffalo, I know just how tough it is. Brad shows flair and knowledge of the game and brings out the minor league atmosphere well in 'Overtime'. As a goaltender, I never like to be scored on in overtime, but for this offering I don't mind seeing the red light go on. It's fun, serious and at times makes you laugh out loud. From the Flames beat to a novel, things have gone well for Brad.

We've both arrived at destinations we once talked about over a long bus ride. Somehow it doesn't seem that long ago.

Dwayne Roloson
Simcoe, Ontario
August 1999

CHAPTER 1

The grass was still wet and trying its best to stay that way, warding off the intense heat from above.

The blazing sun felt like it was a short cab ride away from where he was standing.

Hung over, his head pounded like a jackhammer. That local sport drink he was a spokesperson for just wasn't cutting through his alcohol-induced haze.

Must remember to stay away from those White Russians. The milk was giving his stomach problems, he thought. He might want to stay away from that six pack of beer that he gave in to around five thirty this morning, too. He bounced a golf ball off his forearm and into the air where he caught it. It was just some stupid trick he'd learned long ago, back when every day seemed to be a hot summer day.

That's it for this drinking stuff, he thought. He had to curb that in a hurry. He reached into his shirt pocket and flipped an antacid into his system.

Third one of the morning.

His logoed hat was pulled down hard over his eyes, trying to augment the wraparound Sun Ray sunglasses. Those sunglasses were a product he had wanted to represent. He found out quickly there wasn't much demand for an old minor-league hockey player to endorse shades. Much more fashionable to have them endorsed by some pussy turtleneck-wearing European standing on a ski hill somewhere in the fucking Alps.

Least that's what he thought.

"Fuck the sunglasses contract," he told his agent, who tried to get him a deal once.

That was when he was an up and comer out of Canada's Eastern Junior Hockey League, the roughest and toughest hockey circuit anywhere in the world.

Anywhere.

He couldn't believe he was actually standing on the eighth tee at the Westpark Golf and Country Club on this, a Saturday morning.

He should have been sleeping or banging that broad he'd wheeled just a few hours ago. He had taken her right off her boyfriend's arm, laughing all the way to his sleek MGB, the car that had been restored just for him by some old geezer years ago in exchange for hockey tickets.

Take the tickets, sure, any game you want, just get the damn car ready for me, he remembered thinking. The poor toothless bastard without two dimes to rub together gushed over his on-ice exploits with the Alexandria Lynx, back in the old, what was that league called? Fuck it, didn't matter anyway, the dumb hick gave him the car for tickets in section A, row nine.

The team never won when the old bastard was there either. So he stopped leaving tickets for him. But he still drove the car. And after every game he'd find a piece of paper covered with curses stuck on the car's antenna.

The old bastard had to get some frustration off his chest considering he had to buy tickets to the hockey games now.

Prick.

That's what they called each other.

There he was, though. Ninety minutes ago he was downing headache remedies by the handful, finishing a chipped smoke from his bedside ashtray and downing a quart of that rancid tasting Flex-Thirst drink he always had on hand. He had to tell Becky, Betsy, whatever her name was, not to stick around all day.

Now he stood on the eighth tee. He was listening to some overweight morons who'd paid four hundred dollars just for the pleasure of golfing with him in some ridiculous celebrity golf tournament his agent told him he should attend.

He reminded himself to kick his agent's fat ass the next time he saw the no-phone-call-returning twerp. He pictured Morty Llennef, the two-bit shyster who always had something in his mouth, usually his left or right foot.

Asshole.

He remained on the tee and cringed as the fat moron number one told him he once whacked a drive so far the players ahead of him told him to put a postage stamp on his ball. That's how far it traveled.

Yeah, that was certainly funny, Bob or Todd, whatever the insurance agent's name was. Yeah, that was certainly funny when the same story was told back on the number two tee.

Fucking hammerhead.

All three partners of his were slobs. His curse had been almost audible when the three drew his name last night back in the clubhouse. Just when he was hoping for that trio of nurses to pull his name out of the hat.

Instead that old prick Bailey Timmins, who won some fucking curling match back in nineteen fifty-nine, collected the three RNs. No doubt he was thrilling them now with stories of some inside-out turn he perfected against Norway.

Here he was with the three slobs. At least Mike, or Mark, or whatever the thinnest fat guy's name was, had a bounty of cigarettes in his golf bag.

"Give us another dart there, manny. I gotta give these fucking lungs some exercise before training camp," he said. The slug insurance guys roared with laughter, which they did anytime he spoke, another annoying part of these tournaments.

This would be the last goddamn appearance he'd be making at one of these lame things. Although he would miss the young girls hanging around the gallery... Them he could smile for, afford idle chatter with, tell stories old as dirt that got them all hoping they'd be under his arm tonight.

Back to the slobs. Mustn't keep these guys waiting as he listened to Mike or Mark, or Bob or Todd or Peter or Paul, harken back to the nineteen sixties when they were all linemates on some fucking industrial league team that was so much better than today's hockey, Bobby Orr himself couldn't have played.

Gotta get this over with, he thought through his still-screaming head. Because of the pain in his head and the pains in the ass he was enduring, he was moving the slobs quickly, his golf game right on the money despite his hangover. In the bestball-formatted tournament, they were all using his shots, the three dickheads unable to put together one shot, let alone two.

At the twelfth hole, his oasis appeared.

Parked under a huge tree near the teebox sat a girl on a golfcart offering free beer from the golf tournament's sponsoring brewery. Her tee-shirt did little to conceal her sweater puppets.

Perfect, he thought, even though that beer tasted awful in his books.

Forgetting that no-drinking rule that had booked his brain earlier in the morning, he cracked one of the beers in a hurry and doused it. He cracked beer number two in a hurry, doused it and finally allowed himself to sip the third one under the umbrella and beside the girl. The three slobs paid little or no attention to the free drinks or the pretty young thing serving them up. She told him she was a junior at Syracuse University and was home for summer vacation.

He told the girl he was a little dry and that made her giggle. She was ready to turn over her innocence in a New York minute to the craggy hockey player with the five o'clock shadow. Even though it was only, what, ten forty-five in the morning?

He asked her if her daddy knew where she was. Assured that both daddy and mommy knew her whereabouts, he signed a scorecard and slipped it to her, the autograph accompanied by his home phone number, a solid package deal he thought.

Smiling, he plucked five more beer from the cooler and stuffed them into his golf bag. He had received that golf bag free years ago and the shoes he was wearing were also compliments of a local sporting goods store.

"You're up, buddy," said fat slob number one. Damn, didn't he hate to be called buddy or big guy or hoss.

Thinking he'd rather kick this guy in the balls, he thought better and drilled yet another monster drive into the teeth of the fairway. It was just a short iron shot away from the green and, as usual, another birdie. Assuming the slobs didn't find a way to screw it up.

He looked back and winked at the beer girl, then motioned to his most useful playing partner.

"Give us another dart, big guy," he said, trying to remember the guy's name.

Walking in the now dry grass in the direction of the ball, fat slob number two settled in beside him and, here it came, he thought, asked about this season. Who was going to coach the Blades? Who was coming in? Who was going out? What was going on anyway? He had four season tickets and that automatically made him an expert.

"You know I got to thinking," fat slob number two said as he reached behind him to pull his sickly green golf pants out of his ass crack, "that goddamn goaltender ya had couldn't stop shit, so he's gotta go and you're the only one with balls. Anyone going ta help ya or what? Damn. That old Charlie Calder couldn't coach my daughter's softball team. No wonder they fired his ass."

It continued. The three-hundred-yard walk seemed like an eternity to him. He just wanted to find the ball and shut this slob up for fifty-two seconds.

That's another reason he hated these appearances. He answered question after question about a season still three months away. People wondered if it would be like last year when the Burysport Blades were out of the playoffs around November ninth. They were a horseshit hockey team.

As captain he took the brunt of the blame from the fans, management and the media. He figured the media couldn't tell the difference between the Atlantic Hockey Association they covered and the tiddly winks tournament they should have covered.

Now he had to listen to it on the golf course. He should have been at home ready to go with Becky or Betsy for another round.

"We're going to be okay," he said, cigarette smoke fighting the air in his lungs for space. "We got the two kids coming in and that guy from Germany got out of his European contract, so we're going to be just fine. Just wish they'd be smart and name me coach. I'd straighten out this program in a hurry."

After eleven years in the minors, his best days were so far behind him he couldn't remember how much talent he really did have back then. The high living took its toll surprisingly early.

Coaches now talked about him and his love for the bottle, fast cars and faster women. A suddenly slow game branded him trouble these days at the age of thirty-four. So he liked the odd beer, the odd jack of hard stuff; the women didn't mean much. Hell, there'd been only one woman he'd ever loved anyway. The rest were recreation.

He wondered what she was doing now, his one true love. He shook the cobwebs and came back to his hockey thoughts.

Damn, he'd make a great coach, he mumbled. Especially considering the job Calder did last year with the Blades. He remembered looking at the back of Calder's head on those long, numbing bus trips and wondering how that man became a professional hockey coach.

Damn, he'd watched so many Welcome To... signs over his career he could become a travel agent. Not that anyone in their right mind would want to visit these locations, places colder than a whore's heart in any season.

Hauling in a solid lungful of smoke, he fantasized about the coaching idea, alone in his hopes, when fat slob number three edged over and told him about his sixteen-year-old son who was going to be a hockey star. The kid had torn up his midget league last winter, but the little pussy couldn't skate and chew gum at the same time and wasn't sure if he liked girls.

"Tell him to keep practicing and get 'im on the smokes," he told fat guy number three. This earned yet another harumph of laughter from the morons as he crushed the final beer can from his stash.

Mercifully he and the three slugs chugged up toward the

eighteenth green where a tiny gallery was waiting, although to him it looked like at least five hundred people because he was drunk.

Problem was, as he walked toward the green on the par three after a gorgeous drive with a nine iron, his legs felt like cement and the piss factor was near burst.

Those gathered offered him nice words and applause as he and the three slobs arrived at the green. Many on hand were the same fans who told him all winter he couldn't beat the sweat off their bags when he was on the ice with the Blades.

He holed the putt and acknowledged the applause, telling the spectators to piss off under his breath through his fake smile. He shook the three slobs' hands, saying what a great time he'd had and maybe they should all get together for a round again later in the summer.

Like that was ever going to happen.

He cut through the autograph-seeking crowd quickly, smiling that bullshit smile, and hustled to the bar where he ordered a double Jack Daniels with a slice of lime. He told the bartender to tab it, and with his drink clenched in his right hand, he bolted to the pisser for a little peace and felt the weight of the world leave his kidneys. He had wanted to whiz over the last three holes but couldn't because of the three slobs and the kids who watched from the treelines.

He emerged from the bathroom and heard his name above the din. There was fat slob number one with a cold beer for him, some company for Mr. Daniels. Attached to fat guy number one's arm was a halter-top-wearing, long legged cougar, whose better days were well behind her, but still had the body to turn heads.

"I'd like ya to meet my wife Ardelle. She sure loves ta watch ya play and wondered if maybe she could git your autograph," Bob or Todd or whatever his name was said.

Bob or Todd, or whatever his name was, didn't even clue in when Ardelle slipped the hockey player a piece of paper with her cellular phone number on it, which he quickly tucked into his shirt pocket.

She could come in handy in a few hours, he thought.

Bob or Todd forgot about the autograph request and quickly left the scene when he saw old Bailey Timmins holding court. He was explaining to some poor bastard about the double-raise takeout he executed back in nineteen seventy, or was it seventy-one, at the world curling final against Sweden.

Poor Timmins hadn't had a clear thought in his head since he fell at the national senior championship back in nineteen seventy-nine, banging his noggin against three rocks in the house and then the ice, which forced his rink to forefeit the game. That pissed off the rest of the team, who vowed never again to play with the old bastard and his boring stories.

Timmins was also pissed off that the match against Sweden wasn't on television, either. Those new wave curling pricks even did commercials now. Bob or Todd nodded in steadfast agreement and excitedly asked about the new hogline rules in eager anticipation of the old bastard's answer.

Away from the enlightening curling conversation, he was just about to tell Ardelle what a great body she had when the golf tournament organizer interrupted to see if he would say some kind words on behalf of the tournament.

Drunk, he walked amazingly straight to the makeshift podium which was draped in the brewery's colours. He tapped the microphone and hoped to hell he made sense because he was smashed and it was still only three-thirty in the afternoon.

He thanked everybody for coming and supporting such a worthy cause, even though he couldn't tell a soul in the room what the cause was. And, in reality, he didn't give a rat's ass. There was free beer, lots of women and free seafood.

Somewhere in the drunken speech when he should have stopped talking he told those gathered that the Blades were going to be a kickass team this year and would be even better if he could coach. Boy, he'd turn the cellar dwellers around in a hurry.

The applause poured in for that coaching statement. Fat slob number three yelled from the back of the room that he could coach, play and flood the rink if those sorry-assed Blades could win at least twenty games.

This was good. This summer day was much better than it started. He finally left the podium in search of yet another Jack Daniels.

The headache was long gone, replaced by a great buzz that made the beer-cart girl look even better and Ardelle like she was a teenager again.

Damn, he had those gathered in the clubhouse in the palm of his hand. The media twerp had scribbled furiously throughout the coaching boast he'd made. He was still a star, even though he couldn't stand this town, couldn't stand the people who worshipped him.

He slept soundly that night, assured of his future and in the fact that he had banged the beer cart girl, and Ardelle.

"Do us," they had both said when they arrived at his apartment.

Dutch Felvin proved once again he could still score, any way he wanted to.

CHAPTER 2

The sun made yet another appearance in town Sunday morning. It shone through the thirteenth floor window of Conrad Stanton's lavishly furnished office in the building his late father, the real estate mogul, had left, along with most of his business interests, to his eldest son Stephen.

Stephen was sharp as a tack but knew nothing in life except work when the sun came up, work when the sun went down, a lifestyle that had cost him a marriage and the kids he never saw anyway.

Stephen Stanton had had to find something for Conrad to do. He had never paid much attention to him as a brother when they were kids and he certainly wasn't about to start now, although Dad, on his death bed, had asked him not to let shit-for-brains Conrad ruin the family name.

Stephen believed he could let Conrad run the family hockey team, the Burysport Blades, to keep him busy and out of trouble. The franchise never made much money and, as far as Stephen knew, wasn't much of a team, but Conrad accepted the hockey task with glee, telling anyone who'd listen that he was the owner of the Blades, when in reality he was the acting general manager. Acting being the operative word. Owner, he thought, sounded a hell of a lot better than general manager and he purchased over two thousand business cards with the false 'owner' description.

Conrad tried to make sure he knew what went on with the club every day. He even tagged along on some bus trips last winter, but "Fuck this," he told Danny the bus driver after the second day of a long road trip. "It's too damn cold and I want to get home to take care of business. I'm flying outta here as soon as I can."

The bus driver didn't know shit from puddy anyway and just shrugged his shoulders when told of his plan.

Now at his desk, he was still miffed from last night. He thought he had a woman lined up at some celebrity golf tournament. Huge rack on her. Ardelle was her name, he remembered. He thought she was a future date and assumed she'd dump that fat slob she was with earlier in the day.

Didn't know where she got to. But that wasn't as big a problem for him as watching Dutch Felvin grab the microphone to tell everyone he was going to coach the Blades and turn the ship around.

He wasn't going to let some dumb minor-hockey-leaguer make the call on his team. That really pissed him off.

Pissed him off even more when he opened Sunday's sport page and saw Trace Felder's bylined story telling Daily Star readers that Dutch Felvin was going to coach the Blades and lead them to the promised land.

"Son-of-a-bitch," he bellowed, and banged on his huge mahogany desk that held only a jar full of pens and a humour calendar.

"So Dutch Felvin thinks he's running this team," he fumed. He really had nothing else in his useless life to fume about.

It was Dutch who had sent him a bill from a Blades' rookie party at a local strip club last year, wasn't it? He'd had to shell out eight hundred and seventy-six dollars and never even got a look at the entertainment.

What was he going to do? This was a major reason for panic. Panicking always made him feel like he was doing something worthwhile.

He got out his little green book. He flipped through the perfect pages in the book, untattered because he never really had to call anyone, and punched in the home phone number of

Trace Felder, the veteran sportswriter at the Daily Star, Burysport's daily newspaper.

Trace Felder just returned from the bathroom of his one-bedroom dive after he puked his guts out. He was still pissed off. He had a sweet golf-cart girl lined up at the celebrity golf tournament he covered the day before. He thought he was in, surer than ice in the Arctic, only to watch her put down her drink and run after Dutch Felvin when he gave her a nod that indicated he was leaving.

"Fuck you, Dutch Felvin," Trace muttered, and wiped some hurl off his chin.

Somewhere in that apartment the phone shrilled.

He stumbled over the tiny bathroom drunk-step and managed to glance at the old clock he'd had since grade school that told him it was just after seven in the morning.

"Pretty sure it's Sunday," he thought. He hoped it was anyway, because if it wasn't, he was late for work and that prick boss would be all over his ass for coming in past the required hour reeking of last night's party.

Who could be calling at this hour? The paper was out seven hours ago and not one of the fidgety weekend editors had called him about his bylined story. It was a pretty good one, he thought, especially for a summer Sunday when there was usually little or no news of the hockey team.

The phone continued to ring. It was a portable that was always lost like the television remote control. Where it was, he had no idea.

He finally located the shrilling device under his logoed sweatshirt from the University of Pennsylvania, a school he had never attended, but liked the Nittany Lion logo. People assumed he had gone to Penn State because of all the paraphernalia he had that said Nittany Lions this, Nittany Lions that. He never told anyone the difference, even though he went to a small school where the only sports team was cross-country and you needed your own sneakers to compete.

Grabbing the phone was no easy chore. He tripped over that stupid mutt he had inherited, Lucky or Lucy or some such thing, and fell onto the understuffed cushions on his couch, the same couch he had bought at a yard sale for four dollars, which was four dollars more than he'd paid for the dog, which he got when he broke up with Gina, his girlfriend of seventy-eight days. She had made him choose between her and the beast, which is exactly why he didn't trip over Gina to answer the phone.

He turned the phone upside-right after tripping over the dog, which in turn yawned and found cover under his badly beaten coffee table, the same coffee table he had bought for two dollars and fifty cents at a yard sale his sophomore year in college. "Talk to me," he managed to say into the telephone.

"Trace. That you, Trace?"

"Yeah, it's me."

He looked at the test pattern on the television he forgot to turn off when he staggered home just a few hours ago. He remembered falling asleep before he could find out how his favourite baseball team made out last night.

"Trace, it's Conrad Stanton calling. I want to talk to you."

"Well, that's pretty fucking obvious," was all that he could say.

"Damnit, Felvin was drunk as two men and here you are, quoting him without even asking me about it. I was there. I don't need to remind you I'm the owner of this team. You probably don't need me calling your boss to remind him of that. Do you?

"Do you?"

He cringed as he scratched his balls for the first time that day. Why did he have to listen to some know-nothing hockey team general manager who usually asked what inning it was between the first and second period?

"Dutch was in a public forum and knew exactly where he was and what he was saying, so I went with it," he said, his first real words of the day. "Joe wasn't there and I was. So I got the story and went with it."

Joe of course was Joe Eandella, the radio voice of CPUK, the dimwitted broadcaster who was probably out at some convenience store grand-opening yesterday and missed the celebrity golf tournament.

"That right?" Conrad sniffed.

"We'll see about this. Dutch Felvin is not going to be coaching my hockey team. This year. Next year. Or any year after that. Do you understand me? I know who I want as coach. I'm looking at his resume right now. When I announce it, I'll make sure Joe Eandella hears about it first."

He knew Conrad didn't know the first thing about hiring a coach. But red-eyed or not, he sat upright, his reporter voice going off inside his head, telling him he'd better get to work and find out just who Conrad was on the verge of hiring.

Then he thought about it a second longer.

It would have to wait.

"Talk to you later, Mr. Stanton," he said. "Gotta go work out."

He clicked the phone off, turned slightly to his left and promptly fell asleep. The beer-cart girl showed up in his dream but ran ahead of him, a race he wouldn't win.

"Fuck you, Dutch Felvin," his dream said to him.

CHAPTER 3

The all-too-familiar sounds finally woke Douglas MacLeod for good, kids clanging in the kitchen, fighting over the chocolate-covered cereal.

The television fight would be next. Nine-year-old Douglas Jr. would want to watch the gladiator cartoon. Seven-year-old Annie would clamor for the cute cartoon with the annoying squirrels.

He looked over at the nightstand beside their bed to the fancy clock that had been given to them as a wedding gift all those years ago. It registered eight-eighteen. Catharine leaned over and gave him a light kiss on the cheek. She didn't jump him. That didn't happen much anymore. Not with the kids up before a rooster could shake its cobwebs and not since he had been pretty much forgotten in hockey circles.

Hockey was his one true love. It was the only passion he had known, the only thing that could seduce him.

Catharine left him in bed which was pretty much where he'd been since his days as head coach of the Flatsburg Mustangs ended seventeen months ago.

Later he woke up on his own and came down the stairs of the house they owned outside of Flatsburg. He tussled the kids' hair but told them to keep it down, while he nodded good-morning to his wife. Catharine was still a clockstopper, he knew that, but he saw only grey in a world of colours these days.

He took the paper from the kitchen island where she had been reading it and shuffled through the entertainment section, the classifieds and the obituaries to find the sports section.

"Why do they have to make it so hard to find the damn sports these days?" he fumed. "Isn't that the only thing people read?"

He went right for the statistics page and searched for the transactions list.

It was early summer, but his eyes ignored the baseball, college and football transactions and settled on hockey, hoping to find some other coach who had met a fate similar to his.

Nothing. There was just something about the North American Hockey Association, hockey's big apple, announcing some guy had been named director of marketing.

Big deal.

No coaching jobs out there today.

"That was hardly worth getting up for," he muttered as he tasted the first of what would be seventeen cups of coffee, which for him would be a slow day of caffeine intake. He took the sports section, left the kitchen without a word, and went into his tiny office, leaving Catharine with only the four walls to speak to.

Decorating the office walls were his many citations from years gone by. Trophies, plaques, the picture of his Canadian junior player-of-the-year award and his favourite shot, the one of him scoring the winning goal that gave Canada its gold medal at the world junior championship.

He led the Augustine Rockets in scoring each of the four years he played junior in that small Canadian town where hockey was life.

Another picture, laminated for posterity by his doting mother, showed him all smiles. He was eighteen, flanked by two guys in suits as he put on the sweater of the Dunston Blackhawks. The Blackhawks were the envy of everyone in the NAHA after selecting him first overall.

It was all a dream for him back then. He was the best. He had the best of everything. He centered a line on the Rockets with Dave Hopesboard and Danny Reggoc that destroyed every team in their path. Hopesboard and Reggoc went on to fame and fortune. They were still big names in the hockey world. Reggoc, who couldn't do anything except play hockey, had just won his fifth NAHA championship, even though it was with his seventh team. Hopesboard was assured a future outside the game; he kissed all the right babies and shook all the right hands, just like he did when they were all buddies in Augustine. Neither one of them, who went well behind him in the NAHA draft, ever called him anymore. They were just too big.

He was forgotten.

He had been washed up at twenty. It seemed incredible.

In the dying minutes of his last junior playoff game, his career was cut short by a reckless idiot. In a game that was already decided. Blew out his right knee. After a cheapshot. And the punk never apologized.

He wanted to stay in the game. Hockey was the only thing he knew. The Blackhawks took a little pity on him and offered him a job in their sales office. He lasted twenty-three days in that job.

After that he accepted a job in their scouting department, but that didn't work either.

He left the Blackhawks and wound up taking a coaching job in the lowest rung of the minors. He took a ragtag team of misfits from the basement to the playoffs, though, stunning everyone. Whipped through three rounds and won it all with an amazing post-season run.

Still, the phone didn't ring off the hook with congratulatory messages or job offers to move up the coach's ladder. No one called with even an assistant's job. So he went back to the same team and their measly pay the next year. And damned if he didn't win again.

He was almost cheering up until he looked at the picture that Catharine didn't like him having that he kept as a daily reminder even though it put him in a foul mood. The picture of him being carried off the ice in a Rockets uniform. Just off to the side, his back turned to the ambulance attendants, stood number sixteen, the player who had ended his bright and wealthy future.

"Fuck you, Dutch Felvin," he seethed.

Dutch crashed on his unmade bed, the bed that hadn't been made since his mom visited last summer. He flipped on the television to the all sports channel, nothing else better to do on a Monday morning as he waited for Sonny Rufus to arrive.

He ran his hand through his three-day beard and watched a professional roller hockey league game on television, but his mind wasn't on the game, it was back long ago.

He had been a damn fine hockey player in his youth, growing up in Ship Cove, Nova Scotia, a rare combination of power, fury and offensive talent. He could beat you into submission with his fists or beat you with an individual rush. He certainly caught the attention of NAHA teams playing junior hockey in Canada. He remembered how excited his father had been during those years.

Ship Cove won all kinds of tournaments and even went to American cities and won more. And it was Dutch who led the way.

But he went away.

To the junior Linton Bulldogs.

Scored forty-one goals his first year. What really impressed everyone was that all-time record for penalty minutes. Four-hundred-and-nine. Including thirty-two fighting majors. But he wasn't named rookie of the year. That honour went to some phenom with the Rockets up in Augustine named Douglas MacLeod.

He grinned as he remembered Augustine.

Augustine was special. The Rockets usually played home games on Saturday nights, and considering Linton was just forty-five minutes away, the fans always filled the old Comet Centre. Big on pride. Big on tradition. Big on hockey. And big on disdain for each other.

He loved the little rink in Augustine, and the games were always fun. Hockey wasn't the only reason he loved to play in Augustine. It was the place the only girl he ever loved called home.

She was the daughter of the Augustine team owner. Her father found out about them and quickly put an end to it. Made her promise never to talk to him again. It hurt both of them. Young love sliced in half.

He vowed never to love again. She did the same. And then she started dating MacLeod before his back was turned.

There was Danny Reccog and Dave Hopesboard, but MacLeod was the one he hated the most. He always wanted a shot at that bastard. Oh, how he wanted that! But he could never get past those two bookends, Reccog and Hopesboard. They were always there to step in and take him on.

His last year of junior, Linton faced Augustine in the league final. The winner would represent their league in the Canadian Memorial Cup championship in Regina.

They all wanted to win but Augustine had its way in the series. He worried so much about drilling MacLeod he forgot about his own game and scored just once and assisted on only two.

Then they were in Augustine for the fourth game. One more win and the Rockets would be jetting to Regina for the final.

It was no contest. The Bulldogs were out of the game by the second period. He had been in the penalty box for two of Augustine's power play goals.

The second goal came from MacLeod. After MacLeod scored he shot down the Linton bench with his stick pointed like a shotgun. Blew smoke away from the blade. Stuck the stick in a pretend holster.

He scowled as he left the penalty box and crossed the ice. Vicious insults came at him from the fullhouse at Augustine. He'd heard the jeers before. But somehow, this time, they got through his armour. He was going out of junior hockey a loser.

Augustine was ahead 6-1. The crowd was singing. The Rockets put their big three on the ice - as a gesture of thanks to the fans.

MacLeod accepted a pass in his own zone. Made a couple

of head fakes in neutral ice. Darted through the Linton defence. And fired a rocket past the Bulldog goaltender. It was seven to one with forty-seven seconds left. And MacLeod skated to the corner, hands raised, and waited for his four teammates to come hug him.

Dutch went crazy.

Off the face-off, MacLeod was hanging near centre looking for a hat trick when the puck arrived on the tape of his stick. He had room, and he should have passed off or dumped the puck in the corner for the countdown.

But no, he put his head down and went for a goal.

One more move and he'd be in the open.

Never saw it.

Dutch put all his anger into the hit. It was legal as hell. But MacLeod couldn't get up.

Twenty-nine seconds left on the clock and the arena was silent.

He skated small circles near his bench.

He looked into the crowd where he knew Catharine was sitting. He caught her eye and stared at her intensely.

"Fuck you, Dutch Felvin," she mouthed, gripping her program, the one with a picture of MacLeod on the cover.

CHAPTER 4

"Let's go! You in another world or what?" Sonny Rufus yelled.

As usual he had entered the apartment without knocking. He strode into the bedroom.

They were minor-league teammates years ago in Cincinnati and remained fast friends now that they were still buried in the minors.

Sonny had been fighting a losing battle to retain his once glorious hair, but he made sure he let it grow halfway down his back and always wore a hat off-ice. Today the hat Sonny wore had a logo entitled "Be Nice To Animals, Pat A Hockey Player" on the crest.

Sonny and Dutch were the only two Blades to live in Burysport the entire season and they lived within three blocks of the arena.

"I see you looked after yourself again on the weekend. Damn, you're a mess, Dutchie boy," Sonny said, leaning on the dresser in Dutch's bedroom and re-adjusting his hat. "Tipped a few too many, did ya?"

He got up from the bed and flipped off the boring roller hockey game, knocking a book from the nightstand to the floor and losing his page, even though he hadn't picked up the novel in seventeen days.

"Yeah, things were a little rough, but we're back to normal now," he told his buddy. "Feel like a million bucks. Or at least twenty-five thousand."

Sonny smiled like a butcher's dog. "So, ah, tell me Dutchie boy, when you're coach of the Blades, do I get to play the power play and kill penalties?"

He winced.

"That little speech stirred the fuckin' pot a bit, didn't it?" he said. "Shit, I didn't think that little prick was going to write the story. Then I see it the next day in black and white. Remind me never to talk to that hack again, will ya?"

"Dickhead Stanton was out of whack when he read the piece, I'm hearing," Sonny replied with a smile. "Called Felder and reamed him good, then called you a sack of shit. Going to go see 'im and calm him down?"

"Guess I probably won't be coaching after all, but you and me both know I'd be the guy for the job. And no, I wouldn't put you on the power play. Ya take too fuckin' long to shoot. Besides, I'd want to play defence on the power play and centre, too. There wouldn't be enough room for you with me all over the ice."

Sonny smirked and moved out of the doorway so Dutch could get out into the main area of the apartment.

He again ran his fingers through his beard. He decided against shaving and looked at the mass of newspapers, empty bottles and left over spaghetti that dominated the landscape of his apartment.

"Ready to go?" he asked. "I'm kicking your ass today, my friend."

He grabbed a hadn't-been-washed-since-he-bought-it headband from the kitchen chair, found his tennis racquet and remembered the tennis balls were in the MGB.

"Let's get out of here," he said. "I'm hungry too and it's not going to take long to take you down."

Sonny smiled and re-adjusted his hat.

"Fuck you, Dutch Felvin."

The two of them bolted out of the apartment, down the stairs and headed straight for the Burysport Fitness Centre. The noon-hour women's aerobics class was just about to get under way.

Meanwhile, back at the Stanton Building, Conrad's secretary rummaged through her desk drawer and noticed a brown envelope.

"Damn," she muttered.

That envelope had arrived at least two weeks ago, and when he never showed for work on Friday she had tucked it away in her desk. Finding the white letter opener with the Blades logo emblazoned on the handle, she opened the envelope and pulled out four pages of paper enclosed.

It meant nothing to her.

She grabbed the rubber stamp at her desk and adjusted the date to today's July eighth, and quickly left the office. Her day was done.

Conrad eventually arrived early in the evening and fumbled in his pants pocket to find the key. He looked at his watch. The digital display read five twenty-three.

It was always the same feeling for him when he entered his own office. It was his domain and he felt powerful knowing he had his own desk, chair and washroom.

He went to his window, opened the blinds and stared out at the back of a bank next door. He thought the bank needed a touchup and made a mental note to call someone over there and let them know the outside of their building looked like hell.

Freeing his mind of that problem, he whirled. He loved to whirl when he was alone in the office, like Michael Douglas or Richard Gere - someone anyway - whirled in a movie he watched once. It made him feel important to whirl.

As he turned he noticed some paper atop his desk and his heart skipped a beat. The day wouldn't be a waste after all; there was work to be done.

He was impressed right off the bat that the letter had arrived today. His secretary had stamped it and brought it right in, just like she was supposed to.

"Guess it wasn't that bad she left early after all. She probably had a busy day," he thought, as he glanced at his phone messenger and noticed the red light wasn't blinking. "She probably handled all the calls."

He was even more impressed when he started to read the cover letter, especially the part that said "Dear Mr. Stanton."

He read the letter three times, gleefully devouring the typed words that said, "I know you are a hard-working individual with many other aspects of your occupation taking valuable time, but someone with your intelligence and feel for the game of hockey..." blah, blah, blah.

Conrad smiled and reread that short paragraph of bullshit.

"Someone with your intelligence and feel for the game of hockey."

He finally managed to take his eyes off the ass-kissing words and read through the rest of the resume, but the garble about being a first-round draft choice, a top junior player and head coach of a two-time champion minor league team hardly registered. He fixated on "Someone with your intelligence and feel for the game of hockey."

He had never heard of Douglas MacLeod. He had never heard of the Augustine Rockets and had barely heard of the Dunston Blackhawks, but he had heard enough. He had found the new head coach of the Burysport Blades.

"Someone with your intelligence and feel for the game of hockey..."

He read it once again. This time, with his feet on his big mahogany desk, he knocked two paper clips onto the floor.

He was sky-high.

He was going to make a real decision and he couldn't wait to get the ball in motion.

He was going to hire a living, breathing soul to be the head coach of his, his very own, Burysport Blades.

"Fuck you, Dutch Felvin," he snorted.

Where in hell were those paper clips?

CHAPTER 5

Working Friday nights in the summer was just too much to bear, Trace thought, as he hung up the phone at the Daily Star.

Covering the Blades was something he hadn't expected when he moved to Burysport. He never really knew a lot about hockey. Baseball was his true love, but when the newspaper took him on as a summer student all those years ago, he professed his undying love for hockey.

He was brought back to reality when the phone rang at his desk.

"Trace? That you Trace?"

He knew right away. Conrad always said the same thing and it was annoying as hell.

"Mr. Stanton. How goes the battle? Didn't think I'd be hearing from you again after last Sunday," he said, always gleeful if he could stick a knife in Conrad's neck and twist it a little. "What can I do for you, sir?"

"Trace, let me tell you, I gotta apologize for the way I went on the other day about Dutch Felvin. I was just a little hot under the collar. I've been so busy with the team I took some of that frustration out on you. That shouldn't happen. Last thing I want to do is have the best sports writer I know sour at me."

"That's okay, Mr. Stanton. What can I do you for tonight?"

Conrad let seconds slip away and took a deep breath like he was going to announce who won an Oscar.

"I just wanted to let you know, Trace, that I'll be hiring a new head coach, probably have him here early next week. He's a good one, Trace. I don't know how some of the bigger teams let him slip through, but after some careful planning and processing, it looks like he'll be here. Hell of a coach and hell of a person. Burysport is going to be buzzing about this guy.

"I can't tell you any more because I don't want to let the cat out of the bag. And listen, can you call Joe for me? I called the radio station but he was out at some new garage that just opened."

He cursed under his breath. That prick Conrad had called Joe Eandella first and then called him. To make matters worse, he didn't tell him who the coach was going to be.

"Don't even bother trying to figure out who the coach is," Conrad gushed. "I've got this baby under wraps. When I was talking to him I told him, just in case someone calls not to let on he knew anything."

He wanted to find out where Conrad lived and blow his house up, he was so pissed off.

"Why even bother calling me," Trace wondered to himself, "if you're not going to give me a hand?"

He wanted to break the story, but he knew his editor wouldn't give him the space to write a speculative piece about a new coach for the Blades.

"Thanks, I appreciate the call, Mr. Stanton. Make sure you keep me informed, please?" he told the no-good rotten bastard.

"No problem, Trace. We'll be in touch," Conrad replied.

He hung up and put his head in his hands.

Mentally he went through a list of coaches and ex-coaches he knew were available, but he simply couldn't make a case for any of them to move to Burysport and coach the sorry-assed Blades.

With a sigh he punched in a phone number and let it ring, only to have an answering machine click into gear.

"Hey, this is Dutch. Don't know how you got this number, but leave a message and I'll try to get back to you at my own convenience."

He hung up the phone in a foul mood.

"Fuck you, Dutch Felvin," he muttered.

"Hey Dutchie, we painting this town red tonight or what?" Sonny yelled as he flipped through Dutch's enormous collection of compact discs and settled for Dwight Yoakam's latest.

"Is a five pound pigeon fat?" he replied from the bathroom. He was finally shaving his beard but not before he noticed a few more grey hairs in it.

Sonny shoved the disc into the dusty disc player and tapped his fingers on the table as Dwight Yoakam lit into "The Streets of Bakersfield."

As Dwight continued to wail, Sonny thought he heard the phone ring. He was always eager to jump on Dutch's phone, hoping it'd be a woman so he could pretend to be Dutch, captain of the Burysport Blades, and not some fourth string defenceman.

The phone, in fact, did ring, but Sonny, still hungover, was immersed in Dwight Yoakam's CD pamphlet.

"Fuck Garth Brooks," he said, re-adjusting his hat.

This was great, Douglas thought. He managed to get out of going to Augustine where Catharine and the kids had gone to visit her parents. But he would miss the ego massages her father always gave him, repeating the glorious stories of yesteryear when he was a star with the Rockets.

They never talked about the career-ending injury. They would only talk up until that fateful night about the scoring exploits, the championships, the fact that Douglas could pretty much walk on water if he wanted to.

Still, he would grow tired of it all quickly, and spending two weeks back there would be unbearable.

Instead he remained home and thought about life with the person he loved the most.

Himself.

Catharine was still there for him. Sure, he knew she had wanted to put her public relations degree to use and enter the work field, but he liked it much better that she was simply staying home to be a mother to his children. She was bankable and the kids were great as long as he didn't have to take care of them.

If he drank, perhaps the pain would subside, but he never touched alcohol.

The moody silence was broken by the phone ringing in his office.

CHAPTER 6

"Man, we gotta cut this shit out and bear down for some real training or we're going to be awful when camp starts," Sonny slurred into a draft glass. It was that glass that had been filled at least nineteen times in the last ninety minutes. "We gettin' old, Dutchie my boy. This off-season training program ain't working like it use ta."

Dutch couldn't agree more, as he signaled the bartender to top him up again while he winked at a blonde shooting pool with what couldn't possibly be her boyfriend.

"Yeah, whatever, Sonny. Camp's not for another month and we'll be gettin' serious next week anyway," he said.

He tossed out the straw from his double Jack Daniels and swirled the drink with his index finger. "Besides, do ya think the Blades aren't going to have us playing? They need someone to show the way and we're the ones to do that."

He noticed Sonny had lost all interest in the conversation as he too checked out the blond playing pool with what couldn't possibly be her boyfriend. He looked at his watch and noted it was getting on toward eleven. It was time to get his act together and find company for the early morning hours. He'd have to pull double duty and lend a hand to Sonny, who couldn't pick up a cold, the condition he was in.

He saw Sonny glance toward the doorway.

"Well, look who it is. Look who's decided to grace us with his person," Sonny said through his personal fog.

He looked behind him long enough to see Trace Felder

winding his way through the crowd. He watched the reporter perform a double take at the blonde playing pool with what couldn't possibly be her boyfriend.

"What the fuck do you want, Scoop?" he growled, knowing full well that Trace hated that nickname for reporters.

"I tried to get you tonight, but there was no answer at your place," Trace answered.

He looked over at his bamboozled partner, surprised that Sonny hadn't heard the phone ring at the apartment.

"Old man Stanton called me tonight," Trace went on. "Happy as a pig in shit, saying he was going to name his new coach next week. Wouldn't know who it's going to be, would you?"

"Sure as hell not going to be me because of that horseshit story ya wrote last week," he grunted. "Damn, Scoop, you knew better than to write that." He tried to make eye contact with the reporter but settled for his left shoulder instead. "I was drunk and you went and wrote it. Caused all kinds a shit for me and I don't need that."

He glanced away from Trace just long enough to see some young stud say something to Sonny. Through the noise and smoke, he knew it wasn't polite.

"Jess a second, Scoop," he said. He left his barstool for the first time since a piss break about an hour ago. "Scuse me, son, can I help you with something?"

The young stud looked at him and told him to mind his own business.

"Hey," the young stud said to Sonny, who was trying to make his hand find the beer glass in front of him. "I know who you are and we've got some things to straighten out. My girlfriend said you hit on her the other night. I don't like people hitting on my girlfriend. Do you hear me?"

Problem was Sonny wouldn't have heard a sonic boom at that point. He managed to steer his head in the direction of the young stud, though. "So you're a fan of the Blades, are ya?" he slurred.

With that the young stud gave Sonny a push that sent him

from his barstool to the floor and spilled his full glass of draft all over the place.

In spite of his condition Sonny managed to get to his feet and drill the young stud over a table full of women.

And all hell broke loose.

Dutch shook off nine double Jack Daniels and rushed to Sonny's defence.

Bar fight.

The two friends cleaned house with the young stud and his punk buddies. The kids were no match for hockey players who had forgotten more bar scraps than the kids would ever know.

The bartender paid no attention. He just asked Trace what he wanted to drink.

"Ah, rum and water, I guess," Trace said. He had just dodged a body sent his way.

The fight lasted less than forty-five seconds before the bouncers moved in and rounded up the punk and his friends. They whisked them out the door and hurled them to the street. Sonny shook his head and wondered if the fight could have been prevented had he removed his hat while he banged the punk's girlfriend like she had asked.

"As I was saying," Sonny said, re-adjusting his hat that had been knocked sideways. "As I was saying, we gotta start training pretty soon, Dutchie my boy. We gotta pick it up 'cause we ain't getting any younger."

Dutch nodded in agreement as he looked at his right hand. It was swollen. He plucked some ice out of his drink and squeezed it, which numbed the pain a little.

He looked almost squarely at Trace and resumed speaking, "So Scoop, we're getting a new coach, huh? Well fuck Conrad Stanton."

With that, he collected his tenth double Jack Daniels, steered past Trace and went over to the pool table.

Just minutes later, he left with the blond and a friend of hers.

"Hey, Sonny, let's go," he shouted.

Out of the corner of his eye, he caught Trace watching the double sweep unfold.

"Hey, Scoop," he bellowed. "Print this."

"Fuck you, Dutch Felvin," Trace said.

CHAPTER 7

At the same time that Dutch and Sonny left the chaos behind at the bar, Douglas was wondering why his wife would call him at this hour on a Friday night.

He wasn't really in the mood to talk to her, especially now that the sports news was on television, where he could get caught up on the day's events.

He thought about not answering, but if he didn't pick up, Catharine would worry and call back.

He lifted the receiver and accepted a phone call that would change his life.

"Ah, yeah, I'm ah, looking for, ah, Douglas MacLeod," said an unfamiliar, panicky-sounding voice at the other end of the line.

"Speaking," he said, with a furrowed brow. He wondered who the hell this kook was at this time of night.

"Douglas MacLeod, this is Conrad Stanton calling."

He sat upright in his reclining leather chair. He felt a little dry in the throat.

"Douglas, I'd really like it if you could come to Burysport and discuss with me the possibility of becoming the new head coach of our beloved Blades," Conrad gushed. "I read your resume, and out of all the ones we received, yours stood out like a sore thumb. I had to read it half a dozen times. I couldn't believe someone hasn't snapped you up. I sure as hell hope I'm not too late."

"Well, sir, I'd be honoured to come to Burysport and talk

about coaching," he said. "My schedule is pretty clear these days."

He was looking at one of the pictures of his playing days. "I know you have a heck of an organization down there," he said. "I sure would like to be a part of it. My friends in hockey tell me it would be a great place to coach."

"Well, it's been a tough chore getting the names down to a workable number, but you're certainly in the final select group," Conrad lied. "I just want to meet everyone in person. I think eye-to-eye contact is the best way to interview someone for a job as important as this."

He wondered who he was in competition with.

"If you don't mind me asking, sir, who are some of the other coaching candidates?" he pried.

He hoped he'd get an answer so he could set up personality attacks on each of them when he met Conrad.

"Sorry, Doug, that wouldn't be fair to the other guys. I want the process to give everyone a fair chance. I wouldn't have it any other way and I'm sure you can understand that."

Conrad then went on to laud the city of Burysport, its hockey team and everything else he could think of before he asked Douglas to come to town on Monday for a Tuesday afternoon press conference.

"Press conference?" he asked.

"Ah, ah, a meeting, Doug. I want to have you here for a Tuesday meeting with me at two o'clock," Conrad stammered.

"Sure. Tuesday sounds good. I'll come down Monday night to get familiar with the area," he responded.

"Yes, that would be perfect. My secretary will make a reservation for you at the Burysport Inn. It's just across the street from the arena and just down the street from my offices."

"Sounds good. I look forward to meeting you and getting a look at your fine operation," he said.

"We'll see you Tuesday at two," Conrad returned and hung up.

He immediately called Catharine. It was fifteen minutes to midnight, but that didn't matter. This was important news.

She was pleased with Douglas's opportunity, but they said goodbye without either one of them saying they loved each other. He then dove into his desk drawers and rifled through his collection of hockey magazines. He was searching for an article that covered each professional hockey league's roster. If he was going to be the coach of the Burysport Blades he wanted to see what kind of team they really had.

He froze halfway down the team list.

His finger stopped dead on number sixteen.

His eyes refused to leave the name that was there.

He felt a chill he'd never experienced before.

"Fuck you, Dutch Felvin," he snarled.

CHAPTER 8

Monday dawned a day that would be full of twists and turns in Burysport, a bustling Northeastern American city, home to almost one hundred and twenty thousand people.

The Blades had missed the playoffs the past two seasons and the year before that had been bounced in the first round.

The good fans who once flocked to the Burysport Memorial Complex had witnessed exactly one playoff game in the last three seasons.

The usually patient fans were getting restless.

In his office, Conrad fumbled through one of the closets. He was searching for that damn team banner he could spread across the wall at the media room in the arena tomorrow.

He had hardly slept all weekend after he spoke with Douglas and he had spent most of Sunday preparing his speech in front of his bathroom mirror. He could imagine it all now. The season ticket holders and business community would be at the Memorial Complex to hear him speak. He fantasized about his picture in the paper, his words broadcast over the radio and television network. He would be on the six and eleven o'clock sports segments. He'd have to make sure he taped that all-sports network news hour too. If he could just get his damn VCR to stop flashing 12:00, he might be able to do just that.

He was giddy.

He finally located the banner and shook the dust off it. He noticed that the skate blade that was the team logo was a little tattered. He would have to make a note of that on his things to do list.

Just as he was about to leave, he noticed something in the corner of the closet that pleased him mightily.

There was a stack of little black address books, pens and, lo and behold, a wealth of paper clips.

He couldn't believe his good fortune. He gobbled up a couple of books and snatched at least eight pens and two boxes of paper clips.

He couldn't wait to buy thirty copies of next day's newspaper and leave them for that asshole brother to prove he wasn't a screwup after all.

Meanwhile, Trace Felder entered the office, notebook in hand and approached Conrad's secretary.

"Good morning. Is the general manager in?" he asked, expecting to hear a lame excuse as to Conrad's whereabouts.

"Actually he is in, Trace. I'll let him know you're here."

As she got up to leave, Trace, as he always did, looked at her desk.

What he saw startled him.

There was the note on a pink piece of paper, handwritten, with instructions to book Douglas MacLeod into the Burysport Inn.

"Trace. What can I do you for you today, my friend?" Conrad bellowed, emerging from his office with a smile as big as his head.

Trace wasn't there.

Trace was on the way to his office.

In a hurry.

"What the hell are you talking about?" Conrad barked at his secretary.

"Weird guy," is all she said, with a shrug.

Conrad shrugged his shoulders, too.

CHAPTER 9

Sonny marched into Dutch's bedroom wearing shorts, a Blades' tee-shirt marked XXL and a hat with the inscription On Ice Is Twice As Nice.

"Let's get at 'er, Dutchie boy. The first day of working out has arrived," he announced.

He rubbed his right hand through his stubble and put down the book he had decided to read again after three weeks. "I guess the time has come, hasn't it?" he said. He didn't relish the thought of working out the way he once did. It wasn't like when he was a kid back in Ship Cove and his daddy bought all the weight equipment for him.

He knew he was about a month away from being in any kind of shape whatsoever. He also knew he had a big training camp advantage when it came to experience. While the kids and prospects were running themselves ragged during those two weeks of camp, he knew when and where to hide from coaches, when to coast and when to turn it on.

The first week of camp was pretty much meaningless to a veteran of his stature anyway. He always made sure he was involved. His experience always showed the second week when scrimmages started.

You could hide in the mundane exercise of drills, but you couldn't hide in game situations.

Trips to the bars would have to be curtailed somewhat

for him and Sonny. Both were puzzled nothing had come down the pipe on word of a new coach.

They went to the health club and finished their workouts.

"How's the hand anyway? Bother ya liftin'?" Sonny asked, reminding him about the right-hand that felled that punk kid in the bar brawl.

"Na, it's all right. I never even thought about it until ya reminded me," Dutch said. He smiled at the memory of whacking the punk.

Sonny changed the subject and mentioned to him maybe they should go to the concert tonight down by the water. That country band they liked at a local bar one night last winter was playing and the singer was pretty hot. Both of them nodded in mutual agreement that, yeah, she was a rocket and yeah, they would go to the concert tonight to unwind.

With that, he raised his glass full of water and offered a toast to Sonny.

"To a great summer, to us working out, to a season where we finally win something and to a day where some punk doesn't try to beat your head in for taking his girl," he said.

Sonny lifted his glass of water and clinked glasses.

"Fuck you, Dutch Felvin," he said.

Trace had a skip in his step as he left the Stanton Building.

Once in the parking garage, he started left, then couldn't remember where in hell he had put his car.

He was damn sure he had parked under the tortoise sign. But there was no car there that was even close to his. He wished he had one of those automatic car starters or door openers that a couple of his co-workers had bought. Actually he thought they were ridiculous. He laughed at the little blip the things made when you pressed the button on your keychain and your car suddenly roared to life. He didn't like automatic starters. He didn't like car phones, either. He wondered if people who had car phones actually talked on them in traffic or just listened to nothing and pretended to look chic.

He knew Conrad had a car phone. Prick probably had an automatic starter, too.

His eyes scanned the dimly lit garage. He still couldn't find his car. Finally he remembered it wasn't the tortoise sign at all he had parked under. It was a goddamn rabbit.

"Now, where in hell is the rabbit sign?" he cursed aloud.

After taking the ten cent tour of the garage, he finally located his car and told himself the next time he parked at the Stanton Building he was going to park in one of the blue handicapped zones close to the door.

He climbed into the car quickly and added another tear to the shredded fabric.

He stuck the standard into reverse.

He stalled it.

He refired the engine and wheeled out of his parking spot, coming too close to a cement pillar in the process.

He felt like a mouse in a lab maze. Despite the number of times he'd been to the Stanton Building, he took a wrong turn and drove for the exit against the directional arrows.

He made it just in front of a pissed off old prick in a Lincoln Continental and darted to the toll booth to pay his parking fee. Now if only he could find the damn ticket.

The dimwitted bulb working the pay station couldn't hear for shit, what with Metallica blasting through the headphones he was wearing, and he had seen this act before. He waited for Trace to find that green ticket.

Trace tossed a notepad, three bags of fast-food wrappers and a basketball into the back seat as he frantically searched for the parking ticket. All the while some impatient bastard blared his horn behind him.

Finally he gave up the search and shouted above the Metallica din.

"How much without the ticket?"

"Eight dollars?" replied the dimwitted bulb.

"Damn," he muttered.

He dug through his glove compartment for the wallet he rarely carried, found a crumpled ten dollar bill and gave it to the dimwitted attendant, who took his time giving him change. There were no bills either, all coins. He threw the nickels, dimes and quarters into the change tray.

"I'll need a receipt, too," he shouted, figuring he might as well let the company pay.

The attendant returned a receipt with a smile. No wonder, Trace thought. He knew the kid would pocket the extra six dollars and fifty cents he had just made because yet another driver couldn't find his ticket.

As he finally got everything in order, he opened the sunroof and gave the impatient bastard behind him the finger.

Finally out of the darkness and into the sunlight, he drove the familiar path back to the Daily Star and pulled in. He entered the side door of the Daily Star and made his way to the newsroom where he placed a call.

"Good morning, Burysport Inn," said a pleasant voice at the other end of his phone. "How may I direct your call?"

He spoke confidently. "Could I have the room for Douglas MacLeod, please?"

The phone rang.

Trace's hands got warm.

"Hullo," said Douglas MacLeod.

Click.

Trace hung up.

He dashed over to his desk and grabbed his NAHA Guide and Record Book and popped his head into his editor's office.

The editor lifted his head over the fold of the morning paper. He appeared sour, but he didn't say anything.

"I got it. I've got the coach of the Blades. He's in town," Trace exclaimed.

The editor flipped him a sheet of paper off the fax. It had the Burysport Blades' letterhead and a lengthy statement.

Trace read through Conrad's gibberish until he finally located what he was looking for. The Blades had called a press conference for tomorrow afternoon at two o'clock to announce the new head coach. The letter told those it was intended for not to worry about getting ahead of the team. The new coach would arrive in town at one-thirty tomorrow afternoon.

Conrad had hoped to throw everyone off and he had.

Except for Trace.

The editor picked up his newspaper again and looked at Trace.

"Go to it. I'll need twenty inches," he said.

A slow grin spread across Trace's face.

"Fuck you, Conrad Stanton," he gloated.

Conrad Stanton damn near pissed himself.

Douglas MacLeod was as surprised as hell.

Sonny Rufus let out a slow whistle.

Dutch Felvin cursed aloud and slammed his fist onto the kitchen table.

Joe Eandella was at the grand opening of a new fruitstand downtown.

The Daily Star went against policy on this one. It actually put Trace's bylined story on page one.

The headline, in large boldface type, bellowed "Blades Find Their Man." A subhead told readers the Burysport hockey team had reached into the past and hired former junior star Douglas MacLeod as its new head coach.

Trace had exhausted his research on Douglas. He knew he couldn't call many people for quotes or information. He wanted to keep the scoop for himself.

He was ecstatic when he tuned into the local radio station Tuesday morning to listen to Joe Eandella's early sportscast.

Joe led with a local fastball score and Trace knew he was in. The dumb radio bastard had no idea the Daily Star had broken the story, even though the paper had been out for six hours.

Trace's Blades' story was solid. There weren't any quotes, but it backgrounded MacLeod's career as a player and the unfortunate incident in his last junior game. The story pointed out it was ironic the injury was caused by none other than Dutch Felvin.

He took a moment to muse about how MacLeod and Dutch would get along now that one was the coach and the other a player and finished by saying that the two would have to put their differences behind them for the good of the Blades.

He had no idea of the hatred that existed between Douglas and Dutch.

Conrad was wild.

He had picked up his morning paper expecting to find a nice little announcement indicating the Blades would hold a press conference. Instead he got this.

Everything had been perfect. Not one soul knew about Douglas.

Now all the work, all the time he had spent on himself for the big press conference had been whisked out from under him.

How the hell could Trace ever find out about his big announcement?

He took another glance at the newspaper and noticed MacLeod was spelled with a small 'a'.

Shit. He'd have to change the press release to correct the spelling.

Oh no! He had to call Douglas at once.

"Good morning, Burysport Inn. How may I direct your call?"

"I must apologize for this," squealed Conrad when Douglas answered. "Those goddamn reporters are always a pain in the ass. I couldn't believe it when the story was in the paper. Please..."

He was cut off by Douglas, who had read the Daily Star

with raised eyebrows earlier that morning.

"Mr. Stanton, it doesn't matter to me. All I want to know is if it's true. I tried you at the office last night but couldn't get you and you're unlisted at home. Am I the new head coach of the Burysport Blades?"

"Yes, yes you are, Doug. There isn't a better man for the job. I was just trying to keep everything a surprise," he gushed. He had found his excitement level again and actually toyed with three paper clips.

"We'll meet at the arena a little before the conference so we can actually meet each other," he said before hanging up.

Where was his head?

He had hired a coach he had never met.

Sonny was stunned when he walked towards Dutch's apartment. As usual, he had picked up a copy of the Daily Star that morning but had almost missed the Blades' announcement because it was on the front page, a section he always chucked to the floor.

He had entered his huge bedroom and thrown on some new shorts, with Blades XXL written low on the thigh. He had found a hat that supported his minor-hockey league union and thought about his tennis match scheduled later that day with Dutch.

As he hummed a country and western tune, he returned to the kitchen. Suddenly the sprawled out front section of the newspaper he'd banished to the floor caught his eye.

He saw the headline and pounced on the paper. He drank in the words like cold draft on a hot day.

His day changed.

It was a three block walk from Sonny's apartment to Dutch's place.

He'd let Dutch talk, he thought, as he walked by a newspaper box on the street with that now familiar headline about the Blades. He knew he would have to be reserved.

Dutch talked a lot to him, but it was usually hockey related. One wicked bender, though, he remembered, Dutch had told him about the only girl he'd ever loved. Sonny recalled Dutch telling him that's why he couldn't settle down now and chased women like they were trophies. Sonny had been pretty wrecked that night too. But a lot came back to him. Dutch had told him her father broke up the relationship and then she started to go out with Douglas MacLeod, the same guy whose career Dutch ruined with that hit all that time ago.

Sonny remembered the hit because, like anyone in the game his age, he recalled the offensive exploits and wizardry of Douglas MacLeod.

He remembered that MacLeod was destined for NAHA greatness, and he had even played a junior all-star game against him. Douglas had burned Sonny for a pair of goals that night. But Sonny also knew he had been victimized by one hell of a player, so it didn't really bother him.

Years had diluted the memory of exactly who it was that had ended Douglas's career, but that bender with Dutch a couple of years ago was clear as a picture now.

Dutch was going to be coached by the man he ruined, by the man who had married the only girl Dutch had ever loved.

Sonny knocked on the door of Dutch's apartment.

He had never done that before.

CHAPTER 10

"Fucking agents. That no good, rotten, fat-assed bastard is useless," Dutch roared as he slammed the phone down and motioned Sonny to grab a seat.

He grabbed the crumpled Daily Star and flipped it onto the table.

"Assume ya saw this?" he growled.

"Ah yeah, saw it," Sonny replied. Sonny cleared his throat and re-adjusted his hat.

He barged toward the sink where he put his hands out and leaned against the counter, head down.

Sonny watched his every move.

Dutch looked at his friend but said nothing. The two of them usually knew each other's thoughts, but this day the relationship wasn't working.

Finally Sonny spoke.

"Dutch, I remember ya tellin' me about Douglas MacLeod, only I didn't really click in that it was Douglas MacLeod 'cause we were pretty snapped that night," he said, fighting for words. "I don't know what to say, Dutch. What's going on? What are ya thinkin' over there anyways?"

He pulled up a chair and told Sonny the complete story again. Only this time both were stone cold sober.

"Oh man, I was in love with her," he whispered. "I loved her from the first day I saw her. Then her old man comes in and ends it. Just like that. All over. Then she starts seeing MacLeod after we had told each other we wouldn't love again and would find each other again.

"Yeah, I hit MacLeod that night and pretty much finished him. I never spoke to him again. He was never a friend and now he's come back. He's going to coach here, Sonny. Here, in Burysport. This is my fucking town. I haven't seen him or Catharine since that night. How can all of this be happening?"

All that had felt good about his summer suddenly felt awful.

He told Sonny he had called his agent in Toronto and demanded a trade.

"I dunno, Dutchie. Maybe you should hold off and wait on that part," Sonny said. "You don't need a trade. You don't need to get out of here. You said it yourself, this is your fucking town, man. Maybe you can work this out. It's been a long time. Things change, you know."

"Sonny, I love ya, buddy," he said softly. "But you just don't understand. You don't understand."

Sonny had no idea of the hatred that existed between Dutch and Douglas.

"Don't suppose you're going to the press conference, are ya?" Sonny said and cleared his throat while he re-adjusted his cap for the thirty-seventh time since entering the apartment.

Dutch's glare told him no.

Sonny cleared his throat and re-adjusted his cap for the thirty-eighth time.

Quite a crowd turned out to the press conference. The crowd was much bigger than Conrad had anticipated. He was forced to move the conference out of the media room and onto the concrete floor of the arena.

He had to whiz.

He made a beeline for the bathroom where he quickly rehearsed the lines that were going to bring the house down as he introduced Douglas to the Burysport fans and the media.

Coming out of the bathroom, he shook hands with season

ticket holders. Little did they know he hadn't even washed his hands.

He felt important.

He glided toward the podium that was connected to a long table and noticed that Douglas was shaking hands with the crowd too. Douglas smiled and looked incredibly sharp, dressed in a dark green suit that had obviously cost a lot of money.

The two greeted each other with warm handshakes. Conrad gazed at the crowd.

There was that asshole Trace Felder, wearing a Penn State Nittany Lions' golf shirt. Conrad must remember to remind Trace he was at the big game in nineteen seventy-six when Notre Dame crushed those pricks from Penn State, and how did he like that?

He also saw Joe Eandella on the floor.

All three television stations were there, which was just perfect for him.

He also noticed Ardelle, who was with that fat guy. They were standing close to the head table.

Then the public relations manager of the Blades stepped forward.

Conrad applauded with the others until it finally kicked in that he had just been introduced. His face flushed red and his armpits dripped with perspiration.

He began to speak.

And speak. And speak.

The crowd fidgeted on the floor. Douglas started to play with his tie. Trace stopped his notes, and the television cameras stopped their tape.

Sonny stood at the back of the crowd, wearing a hat that simply said Blades. He shook his head in disgust as Conrad moved to the part of his speech about his college days.

Finally, after twenty-one minutes and thirty-seven seconds he announced, "It's my honour to introduce to you, the new head coach of the Burysport Blades, Douglas MacLeod."

The place erupted.

Everyone clapped.

Everyone except Dutch. He was in the stands alone. In the last row.

"Fuck you, Douglas MacLeod," he muttered.

Conrad couldn't believe the picture in the Daily Star the next day. He had just helped Douglas put on the red and grey sweater of the Blades when that stupid photographer snapped a frame. The picture showed a radiant Douglas with his sweater on and his arms outstretched. His left arm completely blocked Conrad's face.

Trace had done a bang-up job on the story. He had collected the obligatory quotes that Douglas was pleased to be in Burysport and his wife and family looked forward to living in the city. He reported that the new head coach of the Blades promised changes to the Burysport team. The coach said not making the playoffs would be unacceptable and season ticket holders would have a team they would be proud to watch. The new coach would instill a work ethic that would not tolerate lazy play. The Burysport Blades would be the team to beat in the Atlantic Hockey Association.

Sonny was quoted in the story. He said it was nice to see a coach had been named, someone who was obviously qualified and someone who, with the leadership of himself and Dutch Felvin, would work hard to restore pride in the Blades.

Douglas returned to his hotel room after the press conference and called Catharine.

"Sorry, honey. I didn't call you. Things have been so busy. It's been incredible. I got the job. They had a big press conference today and there was a bunch of people here and everything. Sorry I didn't get you earlier. I thought it was too early to call when I first got up and I know you understand. You guys are going to love it here. Burysport is great and I'm going to look for a place tomorrow, but I want you here to make the final decision. This is going to be great. The kids'll love it. There's lots to do."

After most of the arrangements had been made, Douglas remembered something.

"Ah, Catharine, I forgot to tell you," he said. "Dutch Felvin is the captain of the Blades."

Catharine knew that.

It was five weeks until training camp.

CHAPTER 11

Dutch hadn't heard from his agent in a month.

He and Sonny continued to work out, but they rarely went out together because he had grown moody and withdrawn. Sonny even beat him in a tennis match, but the victory didn't feel good.

Sonny finally prodded enough to get him to go out on the town one final night before training camp started. Some of the other players had trickled into Burysport and the boys were ready to get together before they hit the ice.

There were six of them at a table in Brewin's and all of them cheered when he and Sonny entered the bar.

He relaxed a little. The bartender fixed him a double Jack Daniels and lime before he re-joined Sonny and the others, who were exchanging high fives and throwing insults at each other.

The foolishness continued until somebody mentioned the new coach's name. That caused Sonny to put down his draft and Dutch to scowl.

None of the younger players knew of the hatred between their captain and the new head coach, but they knew something was up by his reaction.

Soon the whole table knew, even though they were spared the love interest with Catharine. That would be too much, even though he figured word would be out about that soon enough in the small world of hockey.

He said goodnight and left the bar.

He didn't even glance at the woman who had approached

him.

Just as he jumped into his MGB, Sonny appeared. Dutch looked at his friend and said nothing.

Sonny looked at his friend and said nothing.

He put the MGB into gear and squealed out of the parking lot.

Sonny re-adjusted his hat and went back inside.

CHAPTER 12

Every year it was the same thing in the minors.

Training camp would officially begin with all forty-two players required to sign in and undergo a medical.

Before all of that there was the annual meet and greet with the season ticket holders. They numbered some five thousand this year, over twenty four-hundred of them sold since it was announced MacLeod had assumed command of the Blades.

The social was held at the Westpark Golf and Country Club. Douglas had written letters to all prospective Blades to remind them they would be counted on to be at the social occasion.

None of the players enjoyed the mingling forced upon them by the organization. But none of them wanted to miss it either when they considered Douglas was apparently a hard ass and would frown on someone not being there.

All forty-two players were expected, even if some of them would be part of the first training camp cuts. Most of the players started to arrive at the golf club around six forty-five. All of them lit up when they perused the talent that had assembled.

Douglas was there and he looked sharp in slacks, shirt and tie. The players did a double take when they saw the woman who stood beside him. She was drop dead gorgeous. She wore a short blue skirt which showcased her long tanned legs. She wore her hair in a stylish short haircut which highlighted her large blue eyes, and made her look years younger. She was breathtaking. It didn't take any of them long to figure out she was Catharine MacLeod.

Conrad was there of course. He wondered how much this shindig was going to set him back, but he knew that it would undoubtedly impress Douglas.

He then caught a glimpse of Ardelle, who seemed to be looking for someone, and not that fat guy she was usually with who was instead busy with that old fucking curler. Bailey Timmins was busy with his story of the nineteen sixty-four eastern curling championship where he could have beaten that sorry-assed opponent by himself.

Conrad had met the curler before. He couldn't remember the old bastard's name, but he had promised to honour the old rock thrower before a game some night.

Sure, like that was ever going to happen, he thought to himself.

Sonny arrived. He wore leather shoes, dress shorts and a purple tee-shirt, topped off by a hat that said "Hockey Players Do It In Shifts."

He looked around nervously.

When he had called Dutch to get a lift with him, all he got was the message machine.

When he arrived at the club by taxi, he noticed the MGB was nowhere in sight. It was just a couple of minutes before the social was supposed to start and Dutch wasn't there.

He slid in alongside Trace, who was there to cover the event.

"Seen Dutchie boy, Trace?" he asked.

"No, now that you mention it, I haven't seen him," Trace replied.

With that, his reporter's smoke alarm went off. Before he could make an inquiry, though, Conrad had taken over the microphone, sporting a stain on his shirt from a dropped chicken wing.

Conrad spoke for fifteen minutes and forty seconds, which made Joe Eandella positively ecstatic. It would be great tape for his sportscast, and now he could get out of there. A new cineplex was scheduled to open in just about thirteen minutes. The mayor was going to be there, too.

Conrad's speech bored the hell out of everyone else.

Finally, he introduced Douglas. Those on hand let out a cheer, half for the new coach, all of them because Conrad had stopped talking.

Douglas whipped the crowd into a Friday night frenzy with his plans for the Blades. He told them Burysport would stomp all over its arch-rival the Leinster Monarchs. Pride would be their theme song.

Sonny was even caught up in the excitement. He re-adjusted his hat and noticed the waitress from the bar, who offered him a sweet smile in return.

He also noticed a bright red MGB pull near the clubhouse and its driver fumble to get out of the car.

He forgot about the waitress.

"Shit," he said, and re-adjusted his hat.

He slid away from the crowd and to the door where he met Dutch, who had just come from Brewin's where the bartender had served them up on the house.

Dutch was drunk.

"Dutchie boy. How's it going? What say we blow this place and have a few at my place?" he said.

His words were ignored. He brushed past Sonny like he wasn't even there.

Douglas had just finished his speech and many of the fans had moved toward him to shake the new coach's hand and wish him luck. Including some fat guy who said he sold insurance and introduced his wife Ardelle.

Douglas was smiling, but his expression changed when he noticed a familiar figure moving toward him.

He hadn't seen Dutch since that career-ending night in Augustine.

He flinched. He couldn't remember the last time he

flinched. He felt fear.

Dutch moved closer and Douglas could see he was intoxicated.

He was sure Dutch was approaching him, but he veered off at the last second and stood directly in front of the beautiful woman in the blue skirt.

"Nice to see you, Catharine," he said, his hand outstretched, no smile on his face.

"Oh fuck, Dutch," Sonny muttered and re-adjusted his hat.

Sonny bolted to the front of the room and casually intercepted Dutch from Catharine. He whispered into Dutch's ear that someone needed to see him in a hurry.

He used his strength to steer Dutch away from the former love of his life and away from Douglas. He escorted Dutch out the door wearing a fake smile to indicate everything was all right. He pushed his friend into his sleek MGB and took the keys right out of Dutch's pants' pocket.

He left the Westpark Golf and Country Club behind. He didn't say a word but glanced over at Dutch beside him.

He coasted into Dutch's driveway and shut the engine off.

He re-adjusted his hat and re-adjusted his body to look at Dutch, who had just lit a cigarette. Dutch had stopped smoking about three months ago.

"What in the hell was that all about?" Sonny demanded.

He didn't need an answer and wasn't going to get one.

Sonny and Dutch sat in the MGB until the sun set and gave way to an early September chill.

They didn't talk.

Training camp was twelve hours away.

CHAPTER 13

There wasn't a word exchanged between Douglas and Catharine on the twenty-five minute drive home. As soon as the car was in the garage and the babysitter had left, he started.

He grilled her about the exchange with Dutch at the golf club and threw gasoline on the fire when he told his wife she had shown too much leg anyway.

"You looked like a goddamn groupie the way you were dressed up over there," he roared. "I'm trying to make an impression and you're coming off like a cheap date. What's the matter with you? Why do you do that? Maybe you should have just stayed the hell home with the kids."

"Stop being such an asshole," Catharine said, swiping aside a tear. "Everything's all about you, isn't it? If I wasn't there, you would have said something about that. Everything's always about you, Douglas. Don't give me that public bullshit that fools all those drooling fans. I know what you're like and you're not being fair."

He turned to the coffee maker. He was on a roll.

"Yeah, whatever Catharine. That fucking Felvin shows up like he owns the place and you didn't say a damn word. You just stood there. Everyone saw it. What the hell is that supposed to make me feel like? Tell me that. So you went out with him. Big deal. Guy's a loser. You should have told him off instead of just standing there like a fucking starstruck groupie."

"Douglas, I haven't spoken to or seen Dutch since I was sixteen years old," she blurted. "What? You think I'm still carrying a torch for him or something? I was a kid. We were both kids. What does it matter now anyway? You've got what you wanted. A trophy wife and two kids and you couldn't give a damn about any of us anyway."

That set him off.

"I got what I wanted?" he barked. "What I wanted was to play in the NAHA and I never got that chance, did I? Your old mutt boyfriend took it all away from me. I've been good to you, Catharine, and this is how you repay me, acting like this? Why don't you go check the kids. This argument's over."

He left the room and then stayed up and thought about how much he hated Dutch.

Catharine lay awake in bed by herself and wondered why everything with her husband became an issue. She had no feelings for Dutch. Seeing him had stunned her and brought a rush of memories racing back. But it was over. Wasn't it?

Dutch stayed up and thought about how much he hated Douglas.

Sonny went to sleep with the waitress from the bar who had stopped by and asked him why he wouldn't take his hat off.

CHAPTER 14

The players milled about outside the dressing room, all of them dressed the same in tee-shirts, shorts and flip-flops.

They waited their turn for the medical portion of the camp after they all had registered. Some fine-tuned their hockey sticks with torches, by putting a little more curve in the blade. Some were being fitted with gear by the equipment manager, who listened to them bitch about pants being too large and shinguards not big enough.

After their medicals, all the players had to get their pictures taken by the team photographer, who was also the Daily Star photographer. He cackled his way through the maze of players and tried to make them smile now that they all wore the same uniform. It was the only time some of the stiffs would ever wear a Blades' uniform. Many of them would be gone by the first wave of cuts on either Thursday or Friday.

Dutch had been through this many times before. It wasn't new to him as he sat on the photographer's stool and told the cackler to shut the hell up and get on with it. From there he moved on to get his sticks out of the storage room.

He hadn't seen Douglas but knew he would in about forty-five minutes when the team attended a meeting. There, the laws of training camp etiquette would be forwarded. Despite cautions every year from every coach he ever had, he knew it was every man for himself.

Hell, it was just last year he dropped the gloves with Sonny in a spirited training camp scrap. There were no friends on the ice. That's just the way it was in hockey and it was never going to change. He would fight his mother if it meant he could get to the net a little easier.

The photographer snapped his last frame and the players sauntered into the huge main dressing room. The veterans would dress in the main room for camp. The rookies and other hopefuls would spill into the auxiliary rooms usually reserved for visiting teams.

He entered the familiar room and strode to the soda fountain. He poured himself a glass of soda and cursed because there wasn't any ice.

He crossed the room and found his familiar stall. His name plate wasn't there, instead it was replaced by white tape with his last name written in marker.

His skates were on the floor by his stall. The equipment was laid out perfectly, even though he noticed he'd be wearing number twenty-seven for training camp and not his familiar number sixteen. He was also a member of the green team.

He noticed Sonny wasn't in the main dressing room at all and was actually on the red team, made up mostly of rookies.

That was strange. As he thought about his best friend, Sonny entered the main room and re-adjusted his hat that said simply "Blades Training Camp."

Most of the players had found a seat, and a few leaned against the wall when Douglas entered the room. He wore a Blades' sweatsuit and a team hat.

Conrad was with him. He looked like an idiot in the team sweatsuit and new sneakers he had proudly purchased for over a hundred dollars earlier in the week. They were the same sneakers Douglas wore.

Douglas went immediately to the centre of the floor and left Conrad, who had to search for a place to hide, finally finding a spot between two rookies against the wall.

"You know my name, so I don't have to introduce

myself," was Douglas's way of introducing himself. "This is going to be a tough training camp. If you didn't work out this summer, you're going to be in trouble, I'll tell you that. I run a no-nonsense camp and what I say goes. You have a problem with that, call your goddamn agents and tell them to get you out of here, I don't want you anyway.

"No one is safe on this team. I don't care if you scored 100 points last year in the pros or scored 200 in college," he continued.

The rookies and Conrad listened wide-eyed. Under their breath, the veterans told the coach to piss up a rope.

"You will skate tomorrow in four shifts. Look at the paper on the wall outside of the dressing room to see what time you start. Tomorrow is your last free day until things really get going Monday morning, so I don't have to tell you to stay in tonight and don't let me hear of anyone going downtown. You're all grown men now. You should all understand the next week or so is the most important of your careers."

He felt in control.

"We're going to restore pride in the Burysport Blades and if you want to play here you have to show respect for the uniform, respect for me and respect for your teammates," he said. "That's it. Go home and get rested."

When the meeting broke up, he asked above the din if he could see Dutch in his office.

Dutch glanced over at Sonny and shrugged his shoulders.

Dutch entered the coach's office where Douglas sat surrounded by charts and video tapes. Conrad was there, too, and had just emerged from the tiny bathroom in Douglas's office.

"Have a seat," Douglas said to him. Those were the first words he had spoken to his nemesis since earlier in the game that ended his career.

Douglas turned to Conrad.

"Ah, Mr. Stanton, just wondering if maybe you could leave Dutch and me alone for a few minutes," he said.

Conrad went red in the face and didn't say a word until he reached the door. He told Douglas he'd see him for supper around six.

Douglas checked the door to make sure it was shut and then sat down, directly across from Dutch, who sat with his legs stretched out.

He cleared his throat.

"Listen Dutch, you and I go way back, and we both know what happened that night was stupid. But it happened, and now here we are. Someone once told me hockey's a small world and look at us. I'm coaching and you're still playing. Imagine that?"

He continued. He said the two didn't have to like each other, but they'd have to work together and put aside their personal differences for the good of the Blades.

"I'm not going to lie to you Dutch. I never liked you and I know you never liked me," he continued. "That's okay. We were kids back then and a lot has happened in between. This is my team now. I know you walk on water in this town. I'm not stupid, I've done some checking. I want you to know, though, I'm in charge here. It's my team, not yours. Things are changing around here and you better learn about those changes."

Dutch still hadn't uttered a word.

This was a lecture.

"That's about it for now," he droned. "I hope you understand everything I've said."

Dutch nodded his head and got up to leave.

As his hand reached the doorknob, Douglas spoke.

"Oh and Dutch?" he said in the form of a question. "Don't speak to Catharine again."

CHAPTER 15

This was a pretty good time of year for Trace Felder.

The days were still hot enough to get a tan. The professional football season was just around the corner and his Houston Astros were in a dogfight for a baseball wildcard berth. He had hated that wildcard thing that baseball had introduced. But now that his Astros were in the thick of things, well, maybe this wasn't such a bad idea after all.

Trace was finished with office obligations for another six or eight months. It would probably be six months, because he figured the Blades would miss the playoffs again.

April seemed a long way off, though, as he made his way to the Burysport Memorial Complex.

Training camp was always a special time for him.

It afforded him easy copy. Everyone was accessible for interviews, especially the newcomers to the team who figured a little ink could go a long way in making the Blades.

He wrote a big feature on Douglas to coincide with the opening of camp. He sat in the stands with his notebook in hand as the first group of prospective Blades wheeled onto the ice.

He would usually try and select the Blades' eventual roster after one day of camp. He scratched off names from his list and went position-by-position. He frequently rooted through his Penn State duffel bag which held his life's main support system.

Trace's apartment could be ripped off, his car stolen and his money taken in a heist from the bank, but he could still exist as long as he had his duffel bag. It was complete with a portable computer, power jack, phone line, hockey guides and his phone number book.

Alone in the middle of the lower bowl, he accepted a few catcalls from some veteran Blades who were in the first group. The first crew was kind of a boring mixture the reporter noted to himself. The better, more flamboyant players were in the second and fourth groups.

Just as the digital arena clock ticked nine o'clock, Douglas stepped onto the ice. He joined the players in their lazy laps.

Douglas had been walked to the ice entrance by Conrad who beamed as usual. Trace noticed Joe Eandella was beside the Burysport Blades' self-proclaimed owner.

He smiled to himself and shook his head as Conrad and Joe, two fools, watched practice from rinkside.

He looked through that morning's edition of the Daily Star, where he had a training camp story and a complete list of players complete with mini biographies.

He glanced up from his paper and noticed some of the seats at the Memorial Complex were dotted with bodies.

Some of the players in the second shift had arrived at the rink early, just to see what kind of tactics were going to be used when it was their turn to hit the ice.

Most of them in the stands swilled coffee and were already in their underwear. They watched and observed as Douglas put his charges through the basic rigours of camp. It was about as much fun to watch as a kick in the teeth.

Most players were in better shape these days. They reported to camp already fit.

Trace thought for sure Douglas was going to rip into his players and skate them until exhaustion, but that didn't happen and the puke pool he was in with the trainers was lost.

Used to be, after about seventeen minutes, players were lined up along the boards to empty their stomachs. That fun was all gone now. Things were much more serious.

The players cooled off and stretched at centre ice

following practice. Douglas skated in between to tell them what a great workout it had been. He ordered them to go home and get some sleep to be ready for the afternoon session, even though he hadn't been home in fifty-six hours and had hardly slept. He chose instead to sleep in his office.

Dutch was the first player in the second group to appear by the bench. He watched the ice machine do its work, magically covering the ruts and ridges.

He never liked the first session of camp.

He wasn't in one hundred per cent shape. The early summer outings with Sonny conflicted with his late season fitness regiment, but he was smart enough to know how to get around the physical loopholes.

At least Douglas wasn't a coach who loved the idea of timed runs outdoors and how many pushups a player could do in forty-five seconds.

The guys who always won those endeavours couldn't hit you with a pass if you stood still on the ice, even if they could challenge the Olympic record in the mile run.

He adhered to all the rules Douglas enforced. But he always kept a keen eye on the clock at one end of the rink and waited anxiously for the skate to be over.

With eight minutes left in the session, he coasted to a stop near centre ice for the cool down that signaled the end of the workout.

Douglas had other ideas.

"This might be what you've been used to, Felvin, but things are a little different here this year," he said, and skated little circles around the veteran captain. "You're the star of this team, the captain. Let's show these guys how it's done."

He burned as he did as instructed. He went to the sideboards where Douglas told him to complete ten legburners, which were all-out sprints from one side of the rink to the other.

The other players had gathered in a semi-circle outside

the blueline as his blades dug into the ice. They churned up the roughly eighty-five feet in distance with remarkable ease.

He completed the task and refused to show exhaustion, even though his legs were on fire, heavy and slow to respond.

Douglas wasn't finished.

"Okay captain. Lead the group around, four turns around the rink, stretch, then get off," he shouted, and headed for the exit.

Dutch put his head down and led the players on a well-known tour of the ice. They went around both goal nets, accelerated in open ice and made hard cuts around the corners.

Douglas had stopped under the stands. He didn't say a word. He pretended he was listening to Conrad. It had something to do with the price of oranges. He watched Dutch lead the way. Dutch cursed aloud as he came to a stop to signal the end of practice.

Trace wrote it all down.

He had never seen a player singled out like that on the first day of training camp.

Sonny digested it too, when he found out what had happened, and re-adjusted his helmet. He was out next.

CHAPTER 16

There were no other major interruptions in camp that week except for some heavy hits and a couple of fights.

Dutch hadn't been singled out anymore but was going through camp in an ugly mood. Usually he saved his hits for the exhibition season, but he was running everything in sight and had spent the first four days pretty much to himself. He came to the rink alone and left alone. That disappointed Sonny and in turn had put an edge in his attitude.

Sonny had dropped the gloves with a winger who was supposed to fill the gap in Burysport as the new Blades' enforcer. But Billy (The Kid) Cosman was run out of town in a hurry after his demise at Sonny's hands.

The players still skated in the morning and scrimmaged in the afternoon. All the games were high tempo, which pleased Douglas. There was passion on the ice and that's what he loved to see. Every player refused to give an inch.

The first wave of cuts were scheduled for Thursday and emotions were high as Sonny's team battled the fourth team with Billy (The Kid) Cosman.

Sonny had gone behind the net to start a breakout play when his sixth sense told him trouble was coming from the right. He dished a pass off to his defence partner and caught a blindsided, illegal hit from Cosman that rocked him into the boards. He smacked against the plexi-glass and tore open his upper lip.

He refused to stay down. He got back into the play but

didn't take his eye off the punk enforcer with the big reputation.

The puck eventually came to Cosman on the far boards, but Sonny didn't think about playing it safe. He left the position he was supposed to be in and made a beeline for the winger, who was trying to collect the puck out of his skates.

Sonny's gloves were off at least six strides away from Cosman. He landed a right-left combination to Cosman's face and then kicked the hell out of him. In training camp, the rule is usually no fights. That's one of the biggest jokes in hockey and everyone knew it.

The players stood beside the combatants. They cleared Sonny's gloves and stick away as the defenceman refused to yield to the two officials trying to break up the lopsided fight.

The fight only stopped when Sonny began to tire. He began to tire after he hammered his fists into Cosman's face and head, and that made it clear right then and there that Cosman's expected tenure as a Burysport enforcer was over.

Sonny hadn't even lost his helmet in the one-sided bout. He examined his knuckles that bled on the right hand only, but they were old wounds quick to open.

Dutch smiled when he watched Sonny send Cosman on a one-way ticket to hockey purgatory. Dutch thought he'd better stick around and talk to his good friend when the session was over.

Dutch knew he had moped throughout the first week of camp. That first day when Douglas singled him out had embarrassed him. Despite that he had himself a pretty strong camp, fueled by a lot of bad memories.

Dutch was still trying to locate his agent, but was coming up empty. He wondered exactly what he was going to do.

He had called his father back in Ship Cove after the third day of camp. He was close to his dad, but usually the talk centered around the good times. This was not the good times.

His father told him to put the relationship out of his mind and concentrate on hockey. He told him if he did his job on the ice, there was nothing Douglas could do to him. Don't give him any excuses to make things miserable for the captain. After all

Douglas was the coach, Dutch was the player and there had to be some sort of respect at either end of the spectrum.

Dutch's father had even asked his son if he wanted him to come up to Burysport and stay with him for a couple of days. But with the exhibition games on the horizon, there wouldn't be a lot of time to spend together.

Dutch felt better after that conversation. Douglas didn't put him front and centre after that first workout, and he was flying on the ice. In four scrimmages he had two goals and three assists although he couldn't pick a fight. Players still tended to shy away from him when the going got rough. He knew it wasn't going to be easy with Douglas at the helm, but his father's words were kept snugly in his mind so he relaxed a little.

He waited near dressing room number three when Sonny came off the ice.

"Meet me outside the rink after you shower," was all he said to Sonny, who nodded slowly and pushed the door open.

Sonny let the water soak him hard as he leaned against the centre post in the dressing room shower. The hot stream of water took away some of the pain he was in. It wasn't the fight and the sore knuckles that bothered him, but the overall mass of bumps and bruises that were tattooed all over his body.

He thought he was having a pretty decent camp, although it seemed he didn't have as much time with the puck as he always did. There was always somebody on him when he went to make a pass or retrieve a shoot in from behind the net. As the shower acted as a massage, he put the thought out of his mind that maybe he had slowed down. He'd get it back once the games started for real.

Turning off the taps, he grabbed a towel from the rack. The end of another training camp day had arrived.

The locker beside him had belonged to a kid who had been cleared out while Sonny was in the shower. He was one of eight cuts from that day. Sonny always hated to see players cut.

He remembered the sting he felt when Pittsburgh told him he wasn't good enough to be a regular in the NAHA. He had been taken under the wing of a veteran that first year of camp and always tried to do the same to some of the younger kids who came to the Blades' camp.

He had liked the kid beside him, a defenceman, who was there to try and take his job. For some reason the two bonded and he was saddened to see the empty space beside him. The kid's name on white hockey tape had been peeled from the upper portion of the stall.

He dressed and put a hat on his head with the inscription "Give Blood, Be A Hockey Player" and left the room. He noticed one of the released players was on the public telephone, the same phone that had told countless mothers, fathers, sisters, brothers and girlfriends that the professional dream was pretty much over.

As he shook his head and re-adjusted his hat, he walked outside where he was warmly greeted by sunshine and Dutch.

"Holy shit, brother. You fighting a war or what?" asked Dutch. This time he wanted an answer from him.

He shrugged his shoulders.

"It's nice to see you can still talk, Dutchie boy," he said. "You've been a prick all camp. What's up now?"

"Get in," Dutch answered as he hopped into the MGB. They waved to a couple of players who were walking back to the team hotel.

The MGB settled into the parking lot at Brewin's, where he and Dutch jumped out and made their way through the familiar doors and sat at a table in the back.

Both ordered diet sodas from a waitress they didn't recognize. Neither teammate paid much attention to her anyway. The battles of training camp had dulled their sexual drives.

"Gotta apologize to ya and you know that's something I don't do easily," Dutch said sheepishly. "Haven't been myself trying to figure this game out."

"Hey, I know ya got troubles, Dutchie boy, but that's still

no reason to treat me like a pimple on prom night," he retorted. "Shit, I haven't been able to talk to anyone 'bout anything and that poor kid gets cut today and I don't say a thing to him when I see him talking to his sweetheart back home. Everything's been different around here."

Dutch took a long swallow of soda and signaled for another and a food menu.

"Had a long talk with Dad the other night and he told me some good things," Dutch said. "Told me to suck it up and just play hard, nothing MacLeod can do about that. Can't piss him off any more than he already is. Oh, and how 'bout this? MacLeod told me too, to stay away from Catharine and not to talk to her. Like I'm in junior high or something. Shit, I forgot what a prick he is. Can you believe that? Fucking high school stuff."

He raised his eyebrows.

"See what I'm saying, Dutchie boy?" he said. "You don't talk to me for four days and I miss all this stuff. I gotta know all this stuff so I can help ya. What's he think you're gonna do, nail her down at the rink or something, or what? No wonder ya hate him. Prick hasn't talked to me yet. I can't stand seeing his face."

Both players ordered their food and got caught up on training camp. They compared notes on who was impressive and who wasn't living up to expectations.

"I dunno, Dutchie boy, it feels like I'm slipping or something out there," he said. "Like I'm a step behind or something. You notice anything?"

"Ah, hell, don't worry about it, Sonny," Dutch responded. "Once the real games start, there's no one else we'd want out there. Unless of course it's me, huh?"

"Fuck you, Dutchie boy," sighed Sonny.

CHAPTER 17

The Blades still had twenty-five players in camp as the exhibition season beckoned.

There had been a few surprises late in camp that had the town buzzing. They also had Trace busy with the changes as he informed Daily Star readers who was still with the team, who had been chopped.

Conrad had become involved with the Blades and stuck his nose into places it didn't belong.

He tried to be buddy-buddy with most of the players, but that approach simply did not work.

It had seemed easier to Conrad when he wasn't so involved with the hockey team. He never looked at budgets or payrolls before. Instead he would get his secretary to simply send all the things that appeared costly and difficult down the hall to Stephen. Conrad's older brother never questioned his younger brother and all the bills, as far as Conrad knew, were always taken care of properly.

Not that it was any of his worry.

Now that he was good friends with Douglas, he attempted to learn more about the game of hockey, but the rules seemed foreign to him.

He did know if Douglas told him to jump, he would ask him how high. But he never even noticed he was the head coach's little puppet. He always yielded to Douglas's demands, even though he had been taken aback when asked to purchase three VCRs for the dressing room.

He had stood back amazed as he watched Douglas program the tape machines. The number 12:00 didn't flash on Douglas's VCRs. That had impressed the hell out of him.

There were the usual tears of disappointment and players who second-guessed Douglas's decisions, but the vast majority of cuts were legitimate.

Douglas really hadn't wasted much time trimming his roster. He had been consumed by the Burysport job and he had pretty much cut himself off from the rest of the world.

He had granted several interviews, even though he wasn't overly thrilled with Trace's line of questions. He was especially steamed when he was asked if there could be a problem with no experienced goaltender in camp. That pissed him off because he made the decisions and didn't like someone to second-guess him.

He spent a few days at the office, but decided to return home and even brought a pizza with him the other night for his family to enjoy with him.

He was puzzled when the house was dark and all was silent. Then he noticed it was ten forty-six, so he ate the pizza by himself in his office, poured over strategies and fell asleep on the couch.

He missed his son that morning, who left for school, but he was awoken by his daughter. She had a cold that kept her home and she climbed all over the dad she hadn't seen in a few days.

When he finally came to the kitchen, he thought Catharine seemed moody. She hadn't asked about a thing at training camp even though he told her every detail.

She told him she had applied for jobs and had an interview the next afternoon. He was too busy with a piece of toast to listen and then told her how he had tamed Dutch.

"You should see Felvin now," he sneered. "Anything I ask, he does it right away. I told him face-to-face I wasn't putting up with his bullshit."

Catharine rolled her eyes.

"That's good. We wouldn't want to see you upset," she said sarcastically.

With that, he tossed down the piece of toast.

"I'm outta here," he said. "Tell the kids I love them."

After he left and was on the road to the arena, he remembered Catharine had mentioned about a job interview.

"What the hell is that all about?" he mused.

It left his mind when the thoughts of exhibition games jumped to the forefront. He couldn't wait to climb back behind the bench as the Blades played a pre-season game in two days. They would be at home against the Leinster Monarchs, their arch-rival. He had fantasies about the game, exhibition or not.

He loved the rush fifteen minutes before game time when he entered the dressing room and soaked in all its smells and flavours. He would address the team and go over the game plan.

He forgot to ask Catharine to get his best suit dry-cleaned, but would ask her later that evening to make sure it was ready for him.

As the drive continued, he came back to his wife.

"She hasn't been herself lately," he said aloud. "She hasn't enjoyed any of this."

It never occurred to him that he had had dinner with his family exactly once since camp opened and that had been interrupted with a phone call from Conrad.

As he sat in traffic at a light he wondered a little more about Catharine and her recent attitude. Then he saw a sign that said "Go Blades Go" and promptly thought about the exhibition game and what lineup he was going to use.

CHAPTER 18

The players were excited. There was a difference that day as the remaining twenty-five came to practice. They were in one shift now and all of them knew there were only three or four cuts left.

There was a game tomorrow night against Leinster and even the veterans were upbeat because the Monarchs were the opposition.

Leinster didn't have anything in common with Burysport, but when the Blades won their first championship, it was the Monarchs they defeated in a wild six-game final.

There had been fights and hard hits and dramatic finishes in all six games of that emotional series. It had been almost ten years ago and all of the faces had changed, but when Leinster and Burysport got together, it was super-charged.

Heck, the game tomorrow night was actually just short of a sellout. The people of Burysport were anxious to see if Douglas would change the style of play of their Blades.

Both teams had actually struggled in the league the past few years, but this was hockey in late September against Leinster. Even Dutch and Sonny had anticipation butterflies.

The Blades went through a ninety-minute morning workout and had the rest of the day off before they had to report back for a nine o'clock skate the next morning to go over the lineup.

Dutch and Sonny hooked up with a couple of teammates and went for dinner down at Brewin's. Both had adhered to their long-standing promise not to partake in any partying during training camp. They were both thirty-four and needed every edge they could get. They had listened in envy the other day when players told the story of their hotshot rookie goaltender, who had left the bar with two women on his arm and then stopped pucks like two goaltenders the next morning at practice.

"Those were the days, Sonny. Those were the days," said Dutch. "Remember when we were twenty or twenty-one and stayed out all night, partied, screwed, woke up, threw water on our face and skated like hell in practice?"

Sonny re-adjusted his hat, the one that said "Fear Me" on the crest and smiled at the memory.

"I can't wait for the season to start, Dutchie boy. I've got a serious case of blue balls going," Sonny chortled. "Good stiff wind's all I need right now to get Mr. Oinky going."

The two clinked glasses.

The season would officially start tomorrow night when the players and many of the fans would converge upon the bar after the game.

It was usually the same each season.

If the Blades lost, which was usually the case the past couple of seasons, the crowd was small except for the puck bunnies who made sure their sweaters were tight.

If the Blades won, the crowd was huge and overflowed. The puck bunnies would make sure their sweaters were even tighter.

One of those puck bunnies was just now at the edge of Sonny's elbow and asked him for an autograph.

Through her giggle, the young lady asked Sonny why he always wore a hat and didn't show off those beautiful flowing locks.

Sonny signed her piece of paper, added his phone number and answered the girl's question.

"I don't take my hat of 'cause you'd need it to hold on to, darlin'," he replied.

Dutch shook his head.

"Don't listen to a thing he says, sweetheart," he chimed in. "He's old enough to be your daddy."

He figured Sonny was about to fall off the woman wagon in about four hours. He was wrong. It was exactly five hours when the girl from the bar indeed held onto Sonny's hat, which pissed him off because he had to keep re-adjusting the damn thing.

CHAPTER 19

Dutch was miffed but wasn't overly surprised either.

He wasn't going to be in the lineup that night against Leinster.

It wasn't unusual for veterans not to play in early exhibition games. Douglas told him and four others he wanted to see the younger players perform in game situations.

Dutch, who noted Sonny was in the lineup, was taken aback that Kevin Barrett was going to wear the captain's 'C' that night. He liked Kevin, but it didn't feel right someone else had the captaincy. He missed some games before, but the team always went with three alternates. No one ever wore the 'C' except him.

He and the other scratches stayed out on the ice after the morning skate and did some extra laps, which is what all players not in the lineup on game night were forced to do.

He noticed Trace up in the stands and called him over when the extra fifteen minutes of laps were over.

"What's going on, Scoop? What are ya hearing?" he asked.

"I've heard nothing, Dutch. There's no surprise you're not playing. MacLeod doesn't have to see you play," Trace said.

Dutch decided not to ask Trace if he knew Kevin would wear the captaincy. He wished he had never initiated the conversation.

He told Trace he'd see him around and had to walk past Conrad in the narrow corridor that led to the dressing room. He heard Conrad mumble something about a "big game tonight," but he ignored him.

Douglas was in his office and the message that told him to call home was buried under seventeen faxes and a report on the Monarchs.

He had planned to go home for dinner, but forgot that when the trainer told him goaltender Peter Campbell's groin strain wasn't as bad as initially feared. As a precaution, the trainer told him, maybe backup goaltender Alan Michaels should start, just to be safe.

He was not going to take the advice of a trainer. This was an exhibition game in theory only. He wanted to win and he sure as hell was going to start his top goaltender.

The afternoon went quickly and he noticed the Leinster equipment van had arrived. That got him excited. It was two hours to game time and he felt like it was a championship game.

He loved the smell of the arena on game night. The burnt wood from blades adjusted with a torch, and the odour, that can only be found in a dressing room, that intoxicated him.

The home team sweaters had been laid out in perfect order. The only thing not complete were names on the back, which was Conrad's idea. Douglas sighed when Conrad told him if there were no names on the sweaters, fans would have to buy programs.

He was tiring of Conrad in a big way.

Dutch was dressed in suit and tie which was standard practice for those not in the lineup. But he wasn't down near the dressing room. He had hooked up in conversation with Freddy Benton, the coach of the Monarchs. The two had been teammates for one year together in Buffalo's system and greeted each other warmly on the concourse level of the still empty arena.

"Dutch Felvin, you still playing this stupid game?" said Freddy, hand outstretched.

"Yeah, but not tonight, Freddy. How ya been anyway?" asked Dutch.

The two talked for ten minutes and Freddy lamented the fact that his team would be horseshit. They weren't getting any help whatsoever from that sorry-assed Boston organization, which threw nickels around like they were manhole covers.

Dutch laughed out loud when Freddy made a prediction the Blades would win by five goals because the Polish army had a better defence than he did. Freddy also added his ass would probably be fired in December if help didn't come his way soon.

"By the way, how come you're not playing tonight?" he asked.

"Damn, Freddy, you know MacLeod," Dutch replied. "He told me not to play tonight because he didn't want me scoring five goals."

"Yeah, like you can still score five goals," Freddy muttered.

The two old friends parted with some good-natured jibes and Dutch made his way to the pressbox area where Trace sat.

Joe Eandella was geared up for sound and Dutch listened to him bitch and moan about setting up his broadcast unit which had more wires and headphones than NBC would use to cover the Olympics.

He avoided Trace except for a courtesy nod and went to the players section of the box. He was joined by a couple of teammates, who had a garbage bag-sized portion of popcorn.

Fans started to stream into the Memorial Complex. They looked around to see if much had changed and some pointed at the old AHA championship banner that hung alone above centre ice.

With the building half full, the teams took to the ice forty-five minutes before game time. The sound of loud rock and roll music shook the old building as players stretched and skated their circles and prepared for the pucks and warm-up drills.

Douglas was a nervous wreck down in the tunnel. He had peeked out to see if Catharine and the kids had arrived in their season ticket spots, but they hadn't.

He shouted encouragement as the Blades poured in off the ice and filed into the dressing room. He entered the room and watched some of his players strip off all their gear to towel down.

He reminded them about their roles, what they had gone over in practice and how important this game was to those guys on the bubble who had to impress. The dressing room was stone silent as he went into a college-type rah-rah speech.

It must have worked, as he had his Blades charged. The team throttled the Monarchs six to two in front of over eight thousand fans. His team shredded the Monarchs' defence and Kevin Barrett scored three times much to Douglas's delight.

He refused to let up on his attack. He was ecstatic when his power play unit clicked with thirty-four seconds left in the game to cap the offence.

After the game, he had to endure Conrad's celebration and fended off a hug. Still, he brimmed with excitement. He calmed Conrad down and went back to the dressing room to address his troops before he returned to his office and made up the lineup for the return match the next night in Leinster.

He decided to make a few changes, but Dutch's name still had a line drawn through it.

Catharine and the kids hadn't been at the game. He picked up the phone to call her when the trainer came into his office and told him a rookie defenceman had cramped from dehydration.

The phone call home never materialized.

That night he slept in his office and made a note to call his wife first thing in the morning.

He never made that call either.

CHAPTER 20

The Blades were the early talk of the AHA.

They had swept a home-and-home series with Leinster and outscored the Monarchs fourteen to four before they dusted the Roxbury Colts five to nothing behind a forty-two save effort from Peter Campbell.

They had one exhibition game left at home against the Danvers Hurricanes and Dutch had yet to play a game.

He was royally pissed. He had tried to talk to Douglas but was told not to worry. He was getting itchy and more ornery as each day passed.

After the next day's game against Danvers, the regular season was only four days away. He hadn't seen the ice yet, but he continued to skate extra after practice. He balked at going to the bar with the rest of the gang, even though he apparently missed one hell of a night after the win over Roxbury.

He read Trace's story in the Daily Star which wondered why he wasn't in the lineup.

He knew Douglas was making him stew. It was a small piece of personal payback.

Finally, he received the word from Douglas in a meeting.

"You're going in against Danvers, so be prepared," Douglas told him.

"I've had a lot of time to prepare already," he remarked in return.

Douglas was on cloud nine. No hockey league in the world crowned a champion during exhibition season, but he had his team with three wins and Burysport was behind the new head coach one hundred per cent.

He managed to find time to take Catharine and the kids out for supper, but he spent most of the time signing autographs and chitchatting with fans. Catharine and the kids were all but ignored. He was oblivious of the fact he hardly spoke to his family. He relished hockey talk with the intruders. They would think nothing of plunking a piece of paper down on the dinner table to ask for his signature.

During a brief lull from the autograph signing, he leaned forward and asked her to repeat what she had started to say.

"Well, I've been in touch with the Stanton Group about a job in their public relations department and..."

"Oh, excuse me, honey," he cut in. "Sure I'd love to sign your paper."

He heard her sigh out loud as he scribbled his name for a fan wearing a Blades' uniform.

"Sorry, Catharine," he said. "This is all part of being a coach's wife sometimes. We'll talk about things after dinner when we get home."

He continued to talk about the Blades and by the time dessert arrived, he had told his wife about his game plan for the final exhibition game.

"Well, I'm letting Dutch play, but he's been owly for the last week," he crowed. "You should see him now. He doesn't know if he's coming or going."

He noticed sharply that that caught Catharine's attention.

"I read in the paper where you weren't playing him. How come?" she asked.

"Dutch Felvin has been in this game for a long time and if he can't understand why I'm not using him, then he doesn't know what this is all about," he said through clenched teeth. "He understands the game. I'm the coach. What I say goes. It doesn't matter who it is. Other players haven't played every game either, but he gets all upset about it."

"And what's it all about?" she queried.

He stopped.

He looked into his coffee cup like the answer he needed was at the bottom.

"Dutch Felvin ruined me. We could have had it all if it wasn't for him," he whispered. "Life would be a lot better for me. For us, I mean. He was always jealous of me. He couldn't carry my jock as a player. He's going to learn that I'm still a better person and if he doesn't like it, he can leave. There's going to be some changes around here and if he doesn't like them, tough. Dutch Felvin's a nobody."

He was visibly upset.

Suddenly, their daughter knocked over her drink. It splashed soda on a piece of paper he had on the table that diagrammed plays for the exhibition game.

He never said a word to his daughter. Instead he turned to his wife.

"Have some control over your daughter. She just ruined my notes."

CHAPTER 21

Dutch pulled a hockey stick from the rack. He cuddled it like a newborn and went outside the dressing room to search for the torch to touch up the blade.

He had a ritual. It had been with him since he could remember. He was always the first one in the dressing room on game day. He took grief for that from Sonny, who would never go to the rink with his buddy because it was too damn early. He would get to the arena and grab a coffee from the machine in the dressing room. He would dump a couple of packs of sugar into the cup and walk to his stall. Then he would strip his clothes off and get into his hockey underwear. The underwear was actually a longjohn suit that had the arms cut off and the legs cut off to the thigh.

He never felt comfortable in street clothes when he was in a dressing room. He would get rid of his suit and tie and into his familiar garb to put him in the hockey frame of mind. Then he'd sit at his stall and read the game-day program.

He would drink his coffee and read the program, scanning the opposition roster. This day he didn't recognize as many names as he usually did. The league was younger. Many who had come up with him were now gone from the game. He was a dinosaur, little doubt of that.

After he finished his coffee, he would always stretch for a couple of minutes to get the early kinks out of his system. Then he would fish for his sticks.

He always prepared a new stick for each game, whether

he used it or not. It was always the same method. He started at
the top of the stick and shaved the handle just right for a better
grip. He took a little wood off the tip of his blade before firing
up the torch. The curve on his stick was actually what he liked,
but he always added a little more bend just in case. After the
shaver and torch were put away, he reached for some white tape
and taped the knob, the same way he taped them for years, a
glove length long, a little butt at the top.

He used black tape on the blade and went from the toe
well up the heel. He always liked the look of a well-taped stick.

Then he went back into the dressing room and slid the
new weapon in with the rest of his collection of five sticks.

After an hour on this day some of his teammates trickled
in. Sonny arrived but looked a little weathered Dutch thought.

"What the hell's the matter with you?" he asked. "You
look awful."

"Don't worry, Dutchie boy," Sonny sighed. "Tipped a few
last night. And hey, that instructor from the aerobics class was
something, man. Something else."

He shook his head.

"You know better, Sonny. You know better."

He turned his attention to getting dressed, watching
teammates stretch and focus on the game. He listened to the
music which pounded the four walls. He finished making sure
his elbow pads were snug and fit properly. Then he reached for
his sweater that hung in his stall.

He had just pulled the jersey on and adjusted the arms
over his pads when he noticed the captain's 'C' wasn't there.

"What the fuck is this?" he muttered.

He never said a word but looked across the room at
Kevin Barrett.

Barrett still had the 'C' sewn on his jersey.

He listened to the nervous idle chatter and collected his
stick to join his teammates for the pre-game warm-up. But
throughout the warm-up, he couldn't concentrate. He missed
passes and even ran into Sonny during a three-on-two drill.

"Get your head out of your ass, Dutchie boy," Sonny

yelled. "You tell me I've got problems. C'mon, let's go."

Dutch sidled over to the boards and scanned the crowd. The seats were filling up. He drifted away from the designed warm-up and skated with a puck by himself in the neutral ice. He nodded in recognition at a couple of Danver's players he remembered.

He knew full well Douglas had it in for him. The captaincy switch was just another in a long line of slights.

"Okay, Dutch, screw it," he said to himself. "Just play well tonight. A good game will change things."

Little did he know he wouldn't have a chance to play a solid game.

He didn't start the game and didn't see the ice for the first five minutes. He sat in the middle of the bench, left glove draped over the boards, right glove on his unused hockey stick as wave after wave of player shift changes unfolded in front of him.

The big centre-ice clock ticked down to zero, ending the first period, and he hadn't received a single shift the entire twenty minutes.

He was pissed. He couldn't even congratulate Sonny after he scored off a pretty two-on-one to give Burysport a one to nothing lead.

The second period was more of the same. Line change after line change came and went but never once was he tapped on the shoulder for a shift. He never looked back at Douglas, but his mind raced with emotion. He hated him.

Dutch was aware his teammates even felt uncomfortable now as the second period ended with the Blades ahead two to one. No one said a thing to him as the teams filed back to the locker room.

He accepted a whack on the shinpads from Sonny but didn't acknowledge the gesture to keep his chin up.

Between periods, he listened to Douglas tell the club to drive to the net a little more. He stared at his skates, refusing to look at Douglas and wondered why the coach was so wound up about a meaningless exhibition game.

He noticed MacLeod was starting to lose control and already some players were tuning his style out.

Burysport scored early in the third period and then added another one for a four-to-one lead as the clock ticked down toward the end of the game.

Dutch remained benched.

He had never been this embarrassed before in his professional career.

With just over two minutes left in the game, he watched Douglas lose his temper. The coach ranted and raved at the referee for no apparent reason after a legitimate offside cost the Blades a three-on-two break.

The referee stood beside the Blades' bench and put up a finger of caution to the Burysport coach. Dutch listened as Douglas refused to let up his verbal, obscenity-laced tirade.

The official heard enough. He calmly skated to the scorer's box and assessed the Blades' head coach a two minute minor penalty for unsportsmanlike conduct.

Someone from the Blades had to serve the penalty, which is one of the worst things any player ever has to do, serve someone else's sentence.

Douglas tapped his shoulder and Dutch heard the words that froze him.

"Serve the penalty, Felvin."

The Blades won the game and finished the exhibition season undefeated in four games, but Dutch did not participate in the post-game festivities.

When the penalty he was forced to serve had expired, the game was still on, but he halfheartedly skated to the player's bench, even though the play was in the Blades' end which he knew was a cardinal sin. He counted down the last few seconds and immediately left the bench and went to the locker room while his teammates jumped onto the ice.

He was undressed and in his clothes before the last player came into the room.

He didn't say a word to anyone. He didn't even speak to Sonny, who had added an assist and finished the exhibition season with four points, fourth on the team. He walked into the corridor and blew past Trace.

"Dutch, I just need you for a second," Trace pleaded.

"Fuck off, Scoop. Not now," he snarled.

Trace knew a story when he saw it.

While Joe Eandella and other assorted media types glowed over Douglas and the Blades' fine start, he waited in the background.

When the media scrum ended, he approached Douglas.

"Have ya got a minute, coach?" he asked.

"Yeah, what do you need?"

"Ah, I noticed you didn't use Dutch Felvin tonight and then made him serve a penalty. Something going on here?"

Douglas's smile left his face.

"Look, Mr. Expert, Dutch Felvin doesn't need exhibition games to prove anything to me, and if you want to ask questions, ask him," he shouted. "I needed someone to serve a penalty and he was the one. It could have been anyone. It's only the exhibition season and you're telling me how to run my hockey team?

"There's no story here. Dutch Felvin can handle this. He's a professional. We just won our fourth game in a row and you're worried about someone who didn't play. Maybe you should worry about something else. I worry about my hockey team and that's it. I'll do whatever it takes to win.

"Winning's the bottom line in case you didn't know that. Now, are there any other questions?"

Trace looked up from his notepad.

"Will Dutch Felvin play in the opener?"

Douglas turned on his heels and started for the door before turning back toward Trace.

"Figure it out yourself, Sherlock," he sneered.

Trace closed his notebook and shook his head.

"Asshole," he said to one of the arena attendants. "Now

there's someone who needs a good punch in the head."

CHAPTER 22

Dutch left the arena and drove to a bar he always went to alone, where no one knew him. It was a perfect getaway on the outskirts of town.

He ordered up consecutive Jack Daniels on the rocks and wasted two phone calls on his agent. As he guzzled his drink, he made plans to fire that dickhead agent.

How could all of this have happened? He was in the twilight of his playing days, sure, but he had always thought that his career would finish in Burysport. Probably after two or three more seasons. He had it good here. He was popular with the fans. He didn't pay for much and he had Sonny for company. He was going to have to talk to Sonny and apologize for his actions. Sonny was just too good a friend. He had let Sonny down the past week-and-a-half, but this was a situation he had never gone through before.

He knew Douglas was out to get him, but he couldn't do a thing about it.

Dutch would never quit. He had too much pride for that. He would like a trade, but his agent wasn't helping him at all. He was powerless.

All this was going on in his mind, but the third Jack Daniels started to ease the swirl a little.

He went to the bartender and got some change, which he stuck into a cigarette machine and paid way too much for a small pack. He wanted the company of a good solid drink and a good strong smoke. He could drown his sorrows with both and neither the liquor or the cigarettes talked back.

After the fourth drink, he was getting drunk. He butted his smoke and beckoned to the bartender to mix him another.

The bartender brought the drink over and waved away the money he held out to him.

"Compliments of the lady over there," he said.

Dutch squinted through the dark to see who was there.

She got up from the table, drink in hand, and made her way over to him. She pulled out a chair and sat down with grace and elegance.

"Having a few tonight, are we, Dutch? Surely you're not that thirsty from playing?"

He looked directly into the eyes of Catharine MacLeod.

Dutch was at the age where he didn't shock all that easily. As a professional hockey player, he had witnessed all he could imagine. If he hadn't experienced it first hand, he'd heard about it.

This shocked him.

Being at a loss for words didn't happen very often to him. But at this exact moment he couldn't seem to get his tongue to move. He couldn't get his body to react. So he did what most men do when a beautiful woman sits down opposite them unexpectedly - he knocked over his Jack Daniels. In spite of that he nodded lazily as if he didn't care one way or another if she stayed. In reality he was suddenly aching to know what she wanted from him.

Catharine was wearing a light fall blazer and faded blue jeans with cowboy boots. He watched her settle into her chair.

"Waiting for someone?" she asked, smiling. "If you are, I'll leave."

He still had no idea what to do or say, but he managed to shake his head "no" in response to her question.

There were no further pleasantries exchanged.

"Your husband told me not to talk to you," Dutch got out

at last. "He's probably following you. I haven't played a shift for him yet. If he sees this, I may as well ask the owner here if he needs a new dishwasher."

Catharine smiled again.

Which made him ache even worse.

She had a gorgeous smile. It was the kind of smile that lit up her already beautiful features. It had always made his heart skip a beat. He had loved to see her smile when they were kids. He had shut Catharine out of his life a long time ago, but he had never forgotten her.

He never could.

"Douglas wouldn't know if I was here with you, at home with the kids, or in Timbuctoo screwing the mayor of that city," Catharine said. "He doesn't know what I do from sunup to sundown. He doesn't care either, for that matter."

"I don't remember you ever talking like that," Dutch said. "MacLeod must have the same effect on everyone, does he?"

He traced his left index finger around the rim of his empty glass and signaled for another from the bartender.

He decided to cut to the chase.

"Mind if I ask what in hell you're doing here?" he demanded.

Suddenly he was angry.

"You're here. Your husband hates me. I haven't talked to you this much in twenty years and now you're here, across from me in some dive bar in Burysport. What in fuck are you doing here? Where do you get off following me around?"

He watched her swallow hard and bite her lip.

"I never planned on following you," she said slowly. "I was at the game and I saw what happened. I knew Douglas wasn't going to use you and it wasn't fair. I know what you're like, Dutch. You haven't changed that much. He's out to get you. It drives him crazy that we're even living in the same city as you. You're someone he's never forgotten. Now he thinks it's his turn to hurt you. I know that and I wanted you to know that. It's not fair."

"Yeah, well I have changed," he retorted. "Not that you would know. Last time we talked we were going to find a way to see each other again. Didn't take you long to forget, did it? Nice girl. Yeah, hell. Haven't changed much, huh? What in hell do you know about me? Nothing, that's what."

"You're older that's all," she said. "I watched you in the warm-up tonight. Same routine as always. One full circle in your own end and then to the bench for a drink. Just like you always did. Then you stretch. Left leg first on the boards in front of the bench. You still rock back and forth on your blades and you still take the last shot. You're still the last one to leave the ice."

"That's nice, but who fucking cares?" he snapped. "I want to be alone."

"Dutch, can I at least talk to you for a minute," she asked. "All I'm asking for is a minute. Please? You don't have to say anything."

He scowled but motioned for her to talk as he chewed on the straw from his Jack Daniels. He watched her stare at the ceiling, gathering her thoughts.

"Listen...what happened when we were kids wasn't right. I know that, but Dad had to have his way. You know what he was like," she said quietly.

He rolled his eyes in acknowledgment.

"I loved you, Dutch. For God sake, you were my first. Douglas doesn't even know that."

He was stunned by that admission.

"I was messed up when Dad told me not to see you. I was so lonely. I didn't think that I would ever laugh again. A few weeks later I went on a date with Douglas."

He scowled.

"I was flattered that he asked and I had nothing better to do. Things just went from there. I didn't plan on it."

He rocked back and forth in his chair.

"Maybe I wanted to make Dad happy. I don't know. I've been following this hockey world around all my damn life."

He pushed back his chair from the table but continued to

listen.

"We were obviously over," she pleaded, "but I still looked for your name in The Hockey News. And I always kept track of where you were playing. I couldn't call or anything. I've had to live with your memory through me and Douglas. He still has that picture of you hitting him. I always felt that I owed you an explanation."

He looked at the ceiling lights and then at her.

"I guess I'm not doing such a good job at it," she said. "I rehearsed it in my mind so often over the years, and now here I am screwing it all up. I'm sorry for everything that happened. If I could do it all over again I would do it differently, but a lot of years have passed and I have the kids to think about now. I'm even sorrier for everything that is about to happen. I don't expect you to forgive me, but I'm sorry."

He moved closer to her from across the table. He was angry.

"You came to see me? You came to see me to tell me you're sorry?" he barked. "Well isn't that fucking great?"

"No, Dutch, please don't..."

"No, you wait a second, Catharine. You wait a second. Your father tells you not to see me and you agree. You tell me you'll always love me and five days later I hear you're seeing MacLeod. I never hear from you again. I see you at that stupid team opening and you look at me like I got three heads. Then MacLeod tells me never to speak to you again. Catharine, I loved you like I never loved anyone else. I compared every woman to you. That was a mistake. Damnit, I probably still love you at this very minute and that makes me want to puke."

He downed the rest of his drink.

"And you tell me you're sorry and that you wished things could be different. Well don't do me any favors. Why don't you just take my money for those drinks and get the fuck out of here."

"You were drunk that night at the golf club. What was I supposed to do, fawn all over you?" she fired back. "No, as far as everything else goes, I've already said I'm sorry. You're right.

We shouldn't have been split up, but I was terrified of my Dad. What was I supposed to do? Defy him? God, I was still a teenager. Dutch, I'm not leaving here without the two of us talking this out. I've waited a long time for this chance."

He grabbed his wallet from the table.

"We have nothing to talk about. Dick. Zero. I've gone on with my life. I sure as hell don't need you here all of a sudden screwing me up anymore than I already am. Go back to your husband and stay the hell away from me. This is crazy. What if someone was to come in here? I can't believe I'm even worried about that. What a fucking joke - me worried about being seen in a bar with a beautiful woman."

She bowed her head.

"MacLeod told me never to talk to you and for once in my life I'm going to listen to that prick," he seethed. "I still don't understand why you're here, Catharine. It's not as if anything you say is going to change what happened or what is about to happen. All I know is that whenever you are anywhere near me, my life gets screwed up in a hurry. I sure as hell don't need this."

He fished in his wallet, took out ten dollars and slapped it onto the table.

"Here's for the drinks you bought. Tip the man yourself," he said.

He got up and walked out of the bar. He wasted no time jumping into the MGB. He started the car and turned up the stereo as loud as it would go as he tore off into the night. Not once did he look back.

"Fuck you, Catharine," he screamed over the music.

He arrived home and flung off his tie. He threw down his suit coat and kicked off his shoes.

He started toward the fridge for a beer and remembered there was none. Instead he settled for rum.

He flopped to the couch and turned on the television

before quickly turning it off. He stood up in the middle of his living room. What in the hell had just happened to him?

Catharine had floored him. She was the last person he had ever expected to see.

He hadn't even noticed she was at the game and he was as good as it got when it came to eye checks of the stands for women. He always compared notes between periods with Sonny and the boys, who watched more than the game itself.

Catharine was as beautiful as ever. He wasn't mad at her, but it felt like the walls were closing in around him.

He was mad at Douglas and he took his frustrations out on Catharine.

He went back to that night at the golf club when he knew, even as he walked up to see her, that it wasn't the right thing to do. Thank goodness Sonny had intercepted him before he really got loose.

Now, she came to see him ready to talk about their past. What was it all about?

He had never been through a situation like this and he had no idea what to do about it.

Why?

He asked himself that question one hundred times and then wished he had listened to her. Maybe a talk would have straightened things out. Maybe he could have told her things he had never told anyone before. Maybe he could have let out the emotions he carried for her. He compared every woman he ever had a relationship with to Catharine. Not his one night stands, but some of the women he had actually dated.

It wasn't fair to any of them, he thought now. It wasn't their fault he had been burned because of an overprotective father.

He dated one girl for almost a year once. He thought it was the real thing until one night he called her Catharine over a romantic dinner.

That was the end of that. She had stormed out of the apartment.

He wasn't on the look for love anymore.

It was always fun to go out with Sonny and score with the puck bunnies, but it had started to get old and so was he. It wouldn't last forever.

He knew Catharine didn't track him down to jump in the rack with him. That wasn't her style. That wasn't what she was all about.

Perhaps she just wanted to talk, like she said, and he never gave her the chance.

He quickly banished the idea of a call to her at home. That would be a bright move.

"Ah yeah, hi, is Catharine there?" he imagined himself asking Douglas. He did smile to himself at the thought of Douglas as he passed the phone to his wife beside him in bed.

It was the first time in ages he had smiled.

He knew he wasn't tired, but he also knew he had to be on the ice in less than seven hours as the Blades prepared for their season opener at home in just two days against the Carolina Mudcats.

He would have had a hard time when he saw Douglas in the morning. It would be difficult anyway after he tore out of the dressing room, but his time with Catharine would make it even more difficult to look at his enemy.

He went into his bedroom and didn't bother to turn on the light. He stripped off and sank naked into the messed up bed as he looked at the clock.

It read two twenty-three in the morning.

Beside the clock, the answering machine blinked.

With a sigh, he hit the rewind button and started the messages, five of them in total.

The first one was from his father. The second message was from his agent who told him there were no leads on a trade.

The third message, from a groupie, he erased.

He never even heard the fifth message after the fourth message clicked in.

He was out of his bed in a shot. He dressed quickly and sped down the stairs.

He didn't need the MGB for the sprint to Sonny's

apartment.

He took the stairs to Sonny's apartment three at a time.

He opened the door and peered into the darkness.

He felt spooked.

He said "hello," and noticed his voice cracked.

He turned on the kitchen light. There was a half gallon of rum on the table and an ashtray full of cigarette butts; a necktie on top of a chair.

He went into the room that held a couch, a television, and nothing else.

He went into the bedroom.

It was dead quiet.

On the edge of the bed was Sonny. He didn't have a hat on and his hair flopped over his shoulders.

Dutch couldn't tell if he was drunk or had just cried his eyes out.

It was both.

Dutch sat on the edge of the bed with his good friend and put his arm around his shoulders.

"I'm sorry, man, I'm really sorry," he whispered.

Sonny didn't say a thing. He just nodded his head slowly.

Sonny, the best friend he ever had, had been traded from the Blades to the Leinster Monarchs.

Sonny was at the kitchen table now. He had put on a hat.

If Dutch was in shock for the second time that night, he had no idea where Sonny was.

Sonny had stopped his sobs and started to tell the tale of what had happened that night.

Dutch listened intently.

"I tried to get hold of you, Dutchie boy, but you weren't anywhere to be found," Sonny said. "I thought you'd be at the bar, man."

"No, I, ah, had to get away and blow off some steam," he replied.

Dutch let Sonny explain about coming home and getting a message to call Trace Felder at home.

It was Trace who delivered the bone-jarring news that Sonny had been traded to the Monarchs, one of the worst teams in the AHA.

"Damn, I hear from a reporter that I've been traded. You believe that, Dutchie boy?" said Sonny. "MacLeod has no balls, Dutchie. Stanton has no balls. They could have told me face-to-face, man. I could have taken it. Instead I gotta hear about it from the newspaper guy."

Dutch felt responsible.

He had been worried about Sonny during training camp because he thought he had lost half a step. Then again, Sonny had produced offensively in the exhibition season and played with fire in his gut.

He didn't tell Sonny how he really felt at that moment. He only told his best friend what he wanted to hear.

"It's going to be okay, Sonny," he said. "Hell, you're going to be away from that asshole."

He was worried sick that Douglas had traded Sonny as another ploy to get back at him.

He knew damn well Conrad had nothing to do with the trade because that dickhead couldn't walk and chew gum at the same time let alone decide to make a trade.

"What do you do? What happens now?" he asked.

"Damned if I know," Sonny said. "I tried to get MacLeod at home, but there was no answer and there's no answer at the rink. What am I going to do, Dutch?

"I'm too old for this shit. You'n me, we've been together a long time. I love it here. I was going to stay here. Now this. I'm not going anywhere, Dutchie boy. I'm closing in on retirement. I wanted to stay here, you know, maybe find a job here, that stuff. Then I find out I've been fuckin' traded to Leinster. From a reporter I find out."

He allowed Sonny to go on a tangent as his friend made plans to rip Douglas's eyeballs out at dawn's first light.

He tried to find positive words for his best friend, and

now, former teammate.

"Listen, Sonny. Go to Leinster and play your ass off," he said. "That's the best revenge. Show him he was wrong. Make him eat this trade."

Then he offered some humour.

"Hey, the fans are going to be pissed, and now the women around here will never know why you don't take your damn hat off," he said.

They both chuckled over that.

The clock read four-sixteen.

He was going to have to skate in about five hours and knew Sonny had to take care of business.

They looked at each other.

"Screw it, Sonny," he said. "Let's get some ice and finish this bottle of rum."

They clinked glasses.

"I love ya, Sonny. You're the best," he said.

"Fuck you, Dutch Felvin," Sonny said. "And the horse you rode in on."

CHAPTER 23

That morning the Daily Star headline atop the sports page told readers about Sonny's trade.

Douglas read the copy with keen interest.

He had returned to his office with Conrad after the game the night before and told him he was going to make a trade.

Even though Conrad had begged him to let him announce the trade, the head coach said no. It would have to be him who worked out the details and formalities and made the announcement.

He knew the Monarchs were in the hunt for a veteran defenceman, but Leinster didn't have much to give up in return.

He didn't care.

He knew all about Sonny's lifestyle and knew he was best friends with Dutch.

To get rid of Sonny would cut a hole deep into Dutch's heart, but that wouldn't be the reason he would give to the public.

He received a seldom used winger in exchange for Sonny. He had tried to talk to Sonny that night, but the player was long gone by the time the trade had been finished.

He actually didn't give a shit if he spoke to Sonny. Let him hear about it somewhere else.

He called all the media outlets well after midnight and told each of them how tough it was to make the trade. He said to lose a player like Sonny would put even more pressure on his young defence.

He had slept in his office that night and awoke feeling refreshed. It was still two hours until practice when there was a knock on his office door.

He was prepared for a visit from Sonny.

He wasn't impressed with the shape Sonny was in.

"That's one of the reasons I traded you, Rufus," he said coldly. "You party too much and don't take this game serious enough. You're a bad influence on our younger players. Your act gets old pretty quick."

He watched Sonny's eyes and took a jab in the chest.

"You're an asshole, MacLeod," Sonny blistered. "I'll be back to haunt you. You're a gutless puke. You fucking coward."

"Get out of here before I call security. You're a loser," Douglas snapped. "I never want to see you again. Remember that."

"I'll remember that. Believe me, I'll remember that," roared Sonny.

Douglas watched Sonny leave the Burysport dressing room for the last time.

"Fuck you, MacLeod," Sonny shouted.

He heard Sonny's last remarks from behind closed doors.

CHAPTER 24

That morning was tough on the Blades as they assembled for practice without Sonny. They all knew it could be one of them next.

Sonny was a legend in Burysport. The fans were not at all happy with the trade.

Douglas gathered his players at centre ice and spoke about Sonny and the trade. He wouldn't look at Dutch.

"Listen up, you guys," he said. "This was a trade we had to make. It's going to make us stronger when we need it most. I know Rufus was popular with you guys and that made it difficult to trade him. It happens. We're a better team right this minute because of that trade. Now put it behind you. All of you. It's time to start work."

He then announced the winger traded for Sonny would arrive later that day and be in the lineup for the Blades' opener at home against the Clifton Cavaliers.

He started practice and watched Dutch go through the motions.

And hid a smile from the players.

After practice finished, Dutch was the first off the ice. That rarely happened. He loved the extra time after practice, whether it was to shoot or stand around the boards and talk the latest gossip with his teammates.

The players had pretty much left him alone that day. He wasn't interested in small talk. He was miffed when Douglas gave the line assignments for the season opener that had him on the third line. It was going to be a defensive line.

He knew how to play both ends of the rink, but it was offense that was his ticket.

He had led the Blades in scoring every year he had been in Burysport. Hell, he had thirty-eight goals and forty assists last season. Those numbers had been career lows for him, but he still made the league's second all-star team. He was in on almost a third of Burysport's goals.

After he showered, he went to his apartment and noticed Sonny had left his tennis racket near the fridge. It brought a smile to his face. He wondered what his buddy Sonny was doing now.

Then he thought maybe he should call his dad and let off some steam, but decided against it. He knew if he called home, his father would get upset and end up spending too much money for the trip to Burysport to make sure everything was okay.

Dutch instead called his agent.

There was no answer.

CHAPTER 25

By now things had settled into routine for the Blades. They were the talk of the league, opening the season with four straight wins before they lost two, which led to another four-game win streak.

Burysport was atop its division and the goaltending of Peter Campbell was a big reason why. The rookie had overcome his injury and had played every minute of every game.

Douglas left practice that morning feeling upbeat, but he was sour with Dutch's solid play.

He arrived home early and pulled into the driveway just as Catharine was getting out of her car. She was dressed in a black business suit and carried a briefcase.

"What the hell?" he muttered.

He quickly climbed out of the car.

"Why the hell are you all dressed up?" he demanded. "What's this all about?"

He watched her wince.

"Douglas, in case you forgot, I had my interview today with the Stanton Group," she said. "Do you ever listen? Maybe if you did, you'd remember something once in awhile."

He furrowed his brow.

"Why do you have to do that?" he barked. "Why do you have to always yell back at me? What's this job shit, anyway? Not enough for you to do here? Jeez, Catharine, I'm not at home as much as I'd like to be, and now you're going looking for a goddamn job. What about the kids? You want them at the baby-sitter's all the time? Who's going to be here for them when they get home from school?"

He stormed toward the house and fumbled with the key in the lock. He had started for the kitchen, when he heard her yell.

"I'm sick and tired of you, Douglas," she wailed from just inside the door. "This is it. I can't take any more of this. You're never here. The kids don't even know you. I don't know you anymore. You're all wrapped up with this hockey team and you don't care about us. I'm sick of it. I want to work again. Is there something wrong with that? You're so goddamn arrogant. What? Should I just stay home and be a housewife? Is that what you want? Well guess what? I'm not going to do that. I have a life and the kids have a life. If you don't want to be a part of that, get the hell out of this house."

He turned and charged toward her, pointing his finger.

"No wife of mine is going to be working. Not when there are two kids at home," he spat. "Be there for them. I'm not going anywhere, so get used to it. You're my wife. You won't be working as long as I'm around."

He watched tears stream down her face.

"Well guess what?" she shrieked. "Stephen Stanton hired me today. I start Monday. And do you know the best thing about it? His business owns your stupid hockey team and he has no idea who you are. That makes two of us."

With that he fled to the office in his house.

He was irate. Catharine was going to start a job. He knew she hadn't been happy lately. Maybe, he thought, she would go to work, realize she missed the kids too much and would quit to get back to her quiet life.

He turned on the television and caught the sports segment.

His Blades were ahead in their division with a healthy record of eight wins and two losses and he heard through the media grapevine that he was touted as a genius for his work with the team.

He knew Conrad was ecstatic and Burysport fans had

responded. They had already sold the arena out three times. The Blades, once again, were the talk of the town.

He had come home early that day after practice to prepare for tomorrow morning's trip to Lewiston where the Blades would play the first game of a seven-game, twelve-day road trip. It was the longest trek of the season.

He had to make sure all was in order for the trip where he hoped to win at least five games. He thought that was realistic. The Blades would play twice in Leinster at the end of the trip and the Monarchs had their heads just above water. He had read that that goddamn Sonny Rufus had been a saviour with his solid defensive play and surprising offensive contributions for the Monarchs.

He also wasn't overly thrilled when Conrad decided to come along on the trip, but he knew the owner was full of piss and vinegar to tag along with the Blades.

He had to figure a way to make sure Conrad didn't want to hang around him and get in the way. He was hoping Conrad would palm himself off on someone else.

He left the office for the kitchen to pick up a slice of pizza around suppertime, saying hi to his kids before retreating to his office again.

He studied his notes and scribbled game plans in a notebook before realizing it was suddenly past eleven o'clock.

It was time to call it a night. He left his office and went upstairs to talk to Catharine. He would tell her she could start the job as long as all the arrangements were made for the kids.

She was asleep in their bed.

He shook his head in disgust and walked down the stairs. He would sleep on his office sofa once again.

CHAPTER 26

Three games into the trip, the Blades held their own. They had won in Lewiston, when Dutch scored the winner early in the third period, before they lost to Rochester. Last night's game had been a tie in a rematch with Rochester, which didn't sit well with Douglas, who had watched Dutch score twice. Burysport should have won the game.

The Blades had an off day tomorrow and would leave for Albany in the afternoon after practice.

Douglas knew his players were ready for a party in Rochester. He wasn't surprised the next morning at practice when each and every one of them looked like ten pounds of shit in a five pound bag.

From his makeshift office in the Rochester arena, he listened to the stories and laughter from the night before. He knew the players would let loose, and although he didn't like it much, he understood there was a place for it. He hoped the players would bond together on the road.

He wasn't going to crack the whip and confine the players to their hotel rooms. The team was going well and he didn't want to stir the pot and ruin the early success. He knew he wouldn't get much out of his players today. He had planned on just a forty-five minute skate to get the team out of Rochester as quickly as possible and on the road to Albany where the Capitals waited.

Upon arrival in Albany, he was forced to entertain Conrad as the two went out for supper. He watched Conrad guzzle three expensive bottles of wine and become a blabbering fool, arguing with the waitress when she presented the bill for over five hundred dollars. He grew bored quickly and needed someone to talk hockey with.

He feigned weariness to Conrad, but to be polite sat in the restaurant while the Blades' general manager sucked back an after dinner cigar and polished off another half litre of wine. At one point he had to reach over and point out to Conrad that the table cloth was on fire after an attempt to put down the cigar had missed the ashtray.

The two returned to the hotel together, but he told Conrad he was going to bed. He told him he'd see him in the morning and stepped onto the elevator.

Once in bed, he called home.

"Hey, how are things going?" he asked when Catharine answered. "Everything all right there?"

"Yeah, sure, we're all great back here," Catharine said. "Couldn't be better actually."

It was the first time he had called home since the trip started. Then it hit him.

"Oh, hell Catharine, I forgot," he stammered. "How's the job going? How you making out?"

"You forgot, did you?" she said coldly. "Well, things are working out great. Stephen, I mean Mr. Stanton, has given me a lot of work. It's actually been great. It feels great to be doing something for a change."

He was listening but busy changing the television channels.

"Oh, that's great, yeah," he said. "How 'bout the kids?"

"They've been doing well. I'm home around four-thirty anyway and the baby-sitter's been excellent," she said. "Like I said, things couldn't be any better."

He glanced at the clock.

"So, the team's going strong. How are the fans back home liking it?" he asked.

He actually had to say "hello," when there was no response on the other end.

"Oh, the people think you're the best coach they've ever

had and they're wondering if you walk on water," she snapped. "You're so fucking wonderful."

He sat upright in bed.

"Why do you have to go on like that? We were having our first normal conversation in a month and you get all bitchy on me," he snorted. "I'm just trying to find out how things are going. Everytime I try to talk to you, you go nuts. Can't we even talk anymore?"

"I guess not. Good night, Douglas."

He stared at the phone receiver.

"Isn't this just fucking great," he muttered.

He turned off the television and stared at the ceiling.

"Something's going on with her," he thought. "Things just aren't right. That fucking Felvin has something to do with this. Ever since she saw him, she's been different. We'll see about this act."

He turned off the light, but couldn't sleep.

CHAPTER 27

The Blades were on a roll as they moved into Trenton for a game against the IceLions. The IceLions were a rugged team and there were four fights by the end of the first period in the rough and tumble contest.

The IceLions had scored a shorthanded goal in the first period and then scored on another just two minutes later to give them a two to nothing lead. Burysport had its chances, but couldn't buy a break and was frustrated early in the second when Trenton went ahead by three goals.

Things changed in the second period when the Blades climbed back into the game thanks to some shoddy Trenton goaltending and trailed by a goal as the third period beckoned.

"That's it, that's it," Douglas shouted in the dressing room. "Keep firing away. They're thinking about us now, guys. Pressure their defence. Hit anything that moves. Hey, one more win on this road trip and it's the most successful one the Blades have ever had. Keep working hard. Crash the damn net and rattle that goaltender."

Just over four minutes into the third period Dutch tied the game for the Blades. Douglas had watched him lurk around centre ice and intercept a Trenton pass, going in alone and scoring on a nice snapshot under the crossbar.

The Burysport bench was on its feet, but Douglas never showed any emotion over Dutch's big goal.

Late in the period, though, the long road trip started to take its toll. With five minutes left to play the IceLions swarmed the Blades, putting on extreme pressure, but they couldn't score.

With a minute and a half to go, a Blades' defenceman cleared the puck toward the Trenton zone. Kevin Barrett caught up to the puck and unloaded a long slapshot along the ice that somehow went in.

The Blades led four to three.

Trenton called a time-out and tried to regroup as its fans heaped abuse on the home team. The IceLions sent their toughest player to the ice to stir the pot and make someone in a Burysport uniform pay the price for four straight goals. It was time for the toughguy to grab some poor Blade, beat him like a circus monkey, and get his team fired up enough to go out and score the equalizer.

The Trenton enforcer said something to one of the Blades. It looked like a challenge for a fight off the face-off.

But when the referee dropped the puck, it was Dutch who dropped his gloves and motioned the toughguy to fight.

Dutch waded in without hesitation and the second punch buckled the toughguy's knees. The third punch staggered him even more. He probably never felt the fourth punch which ended the scrap.

The Blades mobbed Dutch after the fight and watched the IceLions retreat like turtles, even though they had been awarded a powerplay when the referee gave Dutch an extra minor penalty for instigating the fight.

That didn't matter. The IceLions never got a shot on goal after Dutch had unnerved the club with his four-punch knockout of their tough guy.

The Blades had scratched and clawed their way back from a three goal deficit. The next day would be an off-day and life was good for the Burysport team.

The dressing room was in chaos.

Until Douglas entered the room.

He strode to Dutch's locker.

"You selfish sonofabitch," he roared. "You could have cost us that game. We get the lead and you gotta go play the hero and fight that kid. They had a goddamn power play and could have tied it. You're like you always were, Felvin. You're selfish. You're in this game for yourself, not for the team."

He watched Dutch, stripped of gear to the waist, stand up.

"What? You wanna say something, Felvin? You wanna say something? You better come up with something good, Felvin," he yelled.

You could hear a pin drop.

"No. I guess I don't want to say nothing. You're right. I shouldn't have got into the fight," Dutch said. "I should always listen to you, Mr. MacLeod."

Douglas lost it.

"You've got no balls, Felvin. You're a goddamn floater. Far as I'm concerned I'm trading your sorry ass out of here," he screeched.

It was Dutch's turn to snap.

He reared back with his right arm and swung a punch that just grazed Douglas's forehead. But before anything more could happen, the Blades stepped in to break it up.

No one said a word.

Douglas stormed out of the room and into his office, but he knew he had become unglued in front of his players.

He replayed the last half hour of his life.

He had quietly seethed behind the bench when Dutch beat the hell out of that supposed toughguy. He had seethed even more when he saw the lift the Blades got from Dutch's quick knockout.

But he was number one. He was the head coach. He would motivate this hockey team. It wasn't going to be Dutch. No sir. It was going to be him.

Now, because of his hatred toward Dutch, his emotions spilled over.

He burned. He was going to get even with Dutch. He had the upper hand now. The ball was in his corner.

Dutch was going to pay.

"You're fucking done, Felvin," he muttered. "You're fucking done. No one throws a punch at his coach. You don't ever throw a punch at me. You'll pay for this. Just like your loser buddy, Sonny Rufus."

He spat on the floor.

"You're fucking done," he repeated, retreating out of the office.

Unannounced, Conrad entered the room.

"Great job tonight, Douglas, great job," he shrilled.

Douglas had had enough.

"Listen, Stanton," he bellowed. "I've fucking had it with you. This is my goddamn team. You keep your fucking nose out of my business. Do you hear me? It's over. I'm running this show. Now leave me the hell alone. Get out."

CHAPTER 28

"Where the hell is Dutchie Boy?" was the first question Sonny said to Trace when he called him at the Leinster Motor Inn. Trace's phone rang about six-and-a-half minutes after the Blades arrived to prepare for their two game series with the Monarchs.

"You haven't heard?" said Trace.

"Heard what?"

"Dutch has been suspended indefinitely by the Blades," Trace said. "MacLeod had a media scrum after the game and told us Dutch had been suspended for insubordination of team rules. That was as far as he would go."

"Well," said Sonny, "what did Dutchie boy tell you?"

"Never saw him, Sonny. He wasn't in the room and wasn't on the bus after the game," Trace said. "Sorry. I just don't know the whole story. None of the guys told me a damn thing. MacLeod got to his players and told us it was all over as far as he was concerned."

None of the reporters assembled at the Trenton game had any idea what unfolded in the steamy, cramped locker room minutes after the game. Douglas's actions had been swift.

He had called Kevin Barrett into his makeshift office in the Trenton arena and explained the situation.

"No player on my team ever confronts me or does what

Felvin did to me," he said. "Maybe I was a little upset, but you
saw how Felvin reacted. It happened in front of everyone. That
is not acceptable and if anyone doesn't like it, they know where
the door is."

He looked at his captain and gave instructions.

"I'm finished with Felvin," he said. "Tell him he's done
as a Blade."

The dressing room, which had been so full of life and
emotion, felt like death.

The only sound in the room was the tape being pulled off
hockey socks and the showers, where players soaked without a
word.

Dutch sat at his stall and watched Kevin Barrett walk
nervously toward him. He looked like a wild man with his beard,
soaked hair and scars.

"What's up, Kev?" he asked.

"Man, coach tells me you're suspended, Dutch," Kevin
said. "Sorry I gotta be the one to tell you. I don't know what to
do, man. We love ya, Dutch. He's starting to lose it on us."

"Hey, listen. You're doing your job," Dutch said.
"MacLeod isn't going to come tell me I'm done. Don't worry
about me. We'll look after things."

He watched Kevin walk away, and seconds later the
trainer arrived with a slip of paper.

He stared at the note in disbelief. With the Blades moving
on to Leinster, he had to stay behind in Trenton at a hotel before
getting a flight out the next morning to Burysport.

One by one the Blades came over to him and slapped him
somewhere on the body. No words were spoken by any of them,
but the admiration was undoubtedly there.

He couldn't remember anything like this.

He was humiliated in front of his peers, in front of his
teammates.

He had decided not to undress completely. He couldn't.

Instead he sat in his locker with his skates still on and stared straight at the floor.

He was certainly used to suspensions, but they had always come from fighting or other aggressive behaviour on the ice. He had never been suspended or personally attacked like he had been by Douglas.

Dutch told the trainer not to worry about the gear, he'd pack it up and take it with him home to Burysport. He felt the eyes of teammates as they glanced back at him.

As the bus rumbled back to the team hotel, he remained seated in the dressing room mess, surrounded by discarded tape and plastic soda cups.

There was no way in the world he was going to stay in Trenton another night.

He stripped off the rest of his gear and showered quickly. He picked up his skates and then put them down. He grabbed his Blades' sweater and tore it to shreds in a fit of rage. He overturned three benches and smashed the bathroom mirror and sink to pieces.

He sat down again and surveyed the damage.

"What in hell is this coming to?" he muttered.

He left the arena by the back entrance, taking only his skates, hailed a cab to the Trenton airport and rented a car. He pointed the car north and headed home.

Not to Burysport.

To Ship Cove.

At least fifteen hours away.

CHAPTER 29

Sonny was stunned at the news about Dutch.

He tried to get as much information out of Trace as he could, but there wasn't much. All he knew was in his story of the game and a column on Dutch's suspension.

"The decision to suspend Dutch Felvin is one that could go a long way in destroying what has been a tremendously successful season for the Blades," he had written. "For whatever reason, Felvin's suspension is top secret stuff. I don't know what happened in that dressing room, but MacLeod's decision to suspend the heart and soul of the Blades is a huge, grave mistake. It's been building for a long time and may be more knee jerk reaction than anything on MacLeod's part. It's not right. In fact, it's downright pathetic."

He made it clear that the Blades were in shock when they returned to their hotel on the team bus without Dutch.

Trace also pointed out that Douglas had traded Sonny and now suspended Dutch. That meant two of the most popular players ever in Burysport's hockey history were out of the lineup.

"Finally, after years of boring, predictable hockey in Burysport, the Blades are doing something in the standings," he wrote. "Felvin and Rufus were easily Burysport's most identifiable players. They lived in the community, they worked hard for the team. Now they're both gone. Who will pick up the slack? How will the fans react? I'll tell you. It's not going to be pretty when the Blades return to the Memorial Complex without

Felvin. And that's a shame."

No one had a clue to Dutch's whereabouts.

Sonny called Dutch's home number in Burysport but got the same answering machine he had heard for years.

He left three messages but received no returned calls.

He felt awful.

That prick MacLeod had really sent a screw into this season. First his trade, now Dutch's suspension.

Sonny started to go stir crazy. He tidied up his hotel room - he would finally get his own place next week. He flipped on the CD blaster on the nightstand and fastforwarded to the fourth song, Home For Sale by Dwight Yoakam.

After he heard the first verse, he clicked the CD player off and jumped up to get his wallet. He thumbed through it and pulled out a piece of paper with a phone number on it.

He let it ring six times before someone answered.

He asked for Dutch.

The voice on the other end wanted to know who was calling, please.

"Ah, it's Sonny Rufus calling, Mrs. Felvin," he said.

"Hi, Sonny. My God, how long has it been since I've talked to you?" said Mrs. Felvin. "Just a second. Dutch is here. He's out back with his dad. He's pretty upset, Sonny. We didn't know who it was coming up the driveway this afternoon. He drove all night and morning and needs sleep, but he's been with his father since he got here. I'll go get him."

He waited patiently on the other end of the phone and imagined the house in Ship Cove.

"Suppose you're calling looking for some lobster or something, huh, Sonny?" were the first words Dutch said.

"Dutchie boy. What in hell is going on?" Sonny asked. "I'm hearing bits and pieces. I been calling your apartment, and then I think you probably ended up going all the way home and I'm right."

"Ah, man, we finally lost it at the same time, Sonny,"

Dutch replied. "I beat the hell out of that punk in Trenton and took the instigator. We won, but MacLeod got on my ass big time after the game. He's there calling me selfish, right in my face, so close I could smell his breath. Then he tells me I'm through. That's where I lost it, Sonny. Took a swing at him and got a piece of him but not enough. Some of the guys jumped in and he freaked. He was all bug-eyed and shit. I knew I was done right there, Sonny. Thing is, he calls Kevin in to tell him I'm suspended and the kid has to come and tell me. Poor bastard. What a year."

"You took a swing at him?" Sonny shrilled. "What the hell do you mean ya just got a piece of him? The Dutch I know would have dropped him right on the floor. Wow, man, that's amazing. What are ya going to do, anyway?"

"I dunno, Sonny," Dutch replied. "I just don't know what's going on now. My agent can't get anything going and I've been thinking I should just hang them up. Hell, I'm thirty-four. I don't know if I can change. Maybe it's time to retire, you know? Maybe I should just move back here. I've got some land here, and you know I always said I'd build a house here by Mom and Dad. It's something to think about."

Sonny erupted.

"What the hell is that?" he bellowed. "You know damn well you can't retire. Quit talking that shit. That's bullshit. You've been producing all year even with MacLeod trying to screw you. You've got too much hockey left, Dutchie boy. Don't let MacLeod get in your head. That's what the prick wants."

"I don't know what else to do, Sonny," Dutch said. "I need time right now. I need time."

"Well, take your time, buddy," he said. "Take your time. Don't do anything stupid right now. Just be patient."

"Yeah, maybe," Dutch said. "Listen, I'm going to get back with Dad, but make sure you keep in touch, Sonny."

"Sure. Listen, Dutchie boy," Sonny said, "be good and be careful. Keep your head up."

CHAPTER 30

Douglas returned home from the road trip early in the morning.

The kids were running wild as he stepped in the door and said hello to a frazzled Catharine.

"Well, it looks pretty busy here," he said. "How is everybody? Did you miss your dad?"

He hugged his children and simply nodded to his wife.

He went to the fridge and found some apple juice, pouring it into a glass. He noticed Trace's column about Dutch's suspension was on the kitchen table.

"So you heard about what happened, did you?" he said. "I did the right thing."

She looked over at him.

"You did the right thing, did you?" she replied. "You've traded one of the most popular players ever in Burysport, and now you suspend Dutch. That's the right thing?"

"Hey, he took a punch at me and that's something that doesn't happen," he sniffed. "I don't care who it is."

"Actually, Douglas, this whole thing has gone too far," she said. "You're trying to ruin Dutch. It's just becoming too much. It's actually becoming sickening watching what you're doing. Why don't you just leave him alone?"

"Why don't you mind your own damn business?" he snapped. "I run the hockey team. I sure as hell know what's going on a little more than you do. Felvin wasn't helping our team with his selfish attitude. That's the bottom line. What are you worried about Dutch Felvin for?"

"Actually, Douglas, you know something?" she said. "I'm tired of talking hockey. I've been working hard and getting positive results from Stephen Stanton. That makes me feel very good, Douglas. I don't need you coming back here and ruining everything. No more hockey. I can't stand it. I'm doing my own thing. I don't need you to do that."

"Fine," he said. "Do your own thing."

CHAPTER 31

Fall turned into winter and Burysport dug out of a massive storm that blanketed the entire region in the third week of December. As the people shoveled out from the snowfall, the talk of the Blades kept many warm.

The weather was the least of Dutch's concerns. He had flown back to Burysport to collect his personal items and his car. Made the nine-hour drive to Ship Cove in seven-and-a-half back in November.

He was skating with the local junior team in Ship Cove to stay in some sort of shape. He also instructed at weekend hockey clinics for the kids and found fun in the game once again.

He also made a trip to Toronto to find his agent, but nothing was materializing on the trade front.

"Guess what, Morty," he bellowed in the agent's office. "You're absolutely useless. I'm firing you. Send all my files to my home address. That's it; we're through."

The agent stammered and stuttered and tried to make up with him, but he would have nothing to do with it.

Still, there was nothing for him. No calls, no deals. He was miserable.

Finally, some news came his way in early January when the Blades bought out his contract. He received a call late one night at his parent's home from Conrad.

"Mr. Felvin, I'm not sure exactly how to tell you this, ah, Mr. Felvin, but you're no longer an employee of the Burysport Blades," Conrad said. "Sorry to have to tell you, but Douglas wanted me to let you know."

"Oh, that's great, Mr. Stanton," he replied. "I appreciate that. I was wondering if you could do something for me."

"Sure, Mr. Felvin, what can I do for you?" Conrad asked.

"Take yourself and MacLeod and jump off the fucking Burysport bridge, you dickheads," he barked. "Have a nice day."

He knew there had been some backlash from the fans when he was suspended, with letters to the newspaper and call-in radio shows, but it boiled over with the Blades winning.

He read about his release in the transactions of the local newspaper the next day. He also took a call from Trace in the afternoon.

"Hi, Dutch, sorry to bother you, but I'm just wondering if I can get a comment on your release," Trace queried.

"Sorry, Scoop," he said. "My time with Burysport is done. Write what you wanna write. I really have nothing to say."

"It's been different here without you, Dutch," Trace continued. "Since you left, and with Sonny gone, it hasn't been the same around the team. There's only one thing I don't miss. I'm just wondering if you could stop calling me Scoop."

"Sure, Scoop, no problem," he laughed. "No problem."

After the conversation with Trace, he went to the garage and uncovered the old snowmobile. He wanted to be alone.

As the old sleigh blasted through the snow, he wondered where his life was going. Where would it go from here?

He drove to his favourite spot in the world, just half a mile from his parents' home on a lake where he had land. He envisioned a house there someday.

He shut the motor off and sat on the seat of the snowmobile and actually started to laugh out loud.

"I'm thirty four-years-old," he shouted to the wilderness. "And I have nothing to show for it."

He flipped up the seat and wondered if it was still there.

It was.

He twisted off the top of the bottle of Jack Daniel's. The

half gallon had been in the snowmobile for at least eight years. This time he threw away the cap.

As he drained the last swallow, he threw the bottle as far as he could.

He wiped a sleeve across his mouth and fired up the snowmobile to return home. He wasn't sure whether he was drunk or mad.

When he arrived home a few minutes later, he noticed a strange car in the driveway.

His parents always had people drop in, so he put the snowmobile in the garage where his father had a bar fridge. He took out a cold beer and snapped off the cap.

His first swill was interrupted.

"Well hell, Dutchie boy," came the familiar voice. "You call this training?"

He nearly choked on his beer.

Sonny stood before him. His once long hair had been chopped off.

He didn't know what to say, he was so surprised.

"What in hell are you doing here?" he managed.

"Hey, it's all-star break and I declined," said Sonny. "Wanted to come down here to see my buddy, and he's hardly said a word to me yet."

Dutch reached back into the fridge and gathered a couple of more beers. He pulled out a package of cigarettes and offered one to Sonny.

"You must be crazy to come all the way up here," he said. "Damn, Sonny, you were going to the all-star game, man. I saw that and almost died laughing. Now you're here instead. You lose your mind or what?"

Sonny raised a beer bottle and proposed a toast.

The two clinked bottles and drank.

Dutch chugged his beer and promptly got up to get two more. He noticed for the first time in awhile the Burysport Blades sticker on the front of the fridge.

"The Burysport Blades," he muttered. "Man, Sonny. It all seems so long ago. I've hardly done a thing since I almost floored that fucking MacLeod. Anyway, I'll just get pissed off thinking about it. What's up with you anyway? You haven't told me why you'd come all the way to Ship Cove, Nova Scotia in the dead of winter."

"Well Dutchie boy, I'm here to tell you I'm on official business," said Sonny. "Tell me this. You're what, thirty-four now? You're broken down. You're half the player ya used to be. You're single and living at home with very little in the way of anything going for you at all. You don't have a team and you're just gonna sit around here, drink your old man's beer and get fat. Probably going to play slo-pitch this summer too, aren't ya?"

Dutch smiled.

It had been the first time in a long time that he had smiled that way.

"Yeah, thinking about building this spring," he said. "That's all that's on my planner now, Sonny. By the way, there's something different about you. The haircut is bad, but there's something else."

Sonny then leaned toward him and pushed his beer bottle out of the way.

He looked right at Dutch, intense like, which made Dutch break out into laughter.

"What the hell is that look?" he asked. "You're creeping me out."

"Dutchie boy, I'm here on a mission. That mission is from the Leinster Monarchs. We want you to sign for the rest of the year. I want you, the coach wants you and the team. We took a vote and they want you. Not like playing is going to interrupt anything here, Dutchie boy. What do ya say? You don't have too much else going for you."

Dutch sobered up quickly. He leapt from the table and ran from the garage.

"Dad," he yelled at the top of his lungs.

CHAPTER 32

Douglas strode to the bench at the Burysport Memorial Complex and looked across the ice into the stands. He always looked at the four seats where Catharine and the kids and one of their friends sat when they attended games. Those seats had been empty for over a month now, but not tonight.

He was surprised to see his wife there with another man, someone he recognized but couldn't immediately identify.

What in hell is this all about? he thought. He motioned for the trainer to come over during the national anthem.

"Who the hell is my wife sitting with?" he asked.

The trainer whispered in his ear it was Stephen Stanton, and the mystery deepened for him.

Why was she with Stephen? Where were the kids tonight?

The whistle brought him back to attention, but between plays he would glance up and see his wife smiling. He rarely saw her smile anymore.

The game was a cakewalk for the Blades. They remained in first place in their division after thirty-nine games. Tomorrow night's game at home would be the exact midway point of the season.

He wasn't thinking about that. Catharine and Stephen had left with around four minutes to play in the game.

He did a little post-game work but quickly left the arena for home. He rarely did that.

He left the office in such a hurry he never noticed the

league FAX on his desk. He never saw the little piece under player movements that announced Dutch Felvin had signed a free agent contract with Leinster.

He left the arena and drove through the quiet streets for home. Catharine's car was in the garage.

He entered the house and followed the sound of the television, where he found Catharine watching the local news in the living room.

"Hey, you're up late tonight," he said.

"I went to the game, so I'm just unwinding a bit. Your guys played well again," she said.

"You went to the game tonight?" he lied. "I'm sorry, I didn't see you. Did the kids go with you?"

"No, actually I got a baby-sitter and went to the game with my boss, who, I guess, is your boss too," she replied.

"You went to the game with Conrad Stanton?" he continued.

"No, Douglas. I went to the game with Stephen Stanton. If you'd listen sometimes to what I tell you, you'd know Stephen Stanton is my boss," she retorted.

"Oh, I see," he said menacingly. "Should I be concerned that you're going to hockey games with your boss and not telling me about it?"

"No you should not," she said swiftly. "He owns the team, Douglas. He doesn't go to many games. Stephen just found out about the connection between you and me last fall. He asked me this afternoon if I wanted to go and I said sure. I haven't been to many games, either. Or perhaps you haven't noticed."

"I see you call him Stephen," he muttered.

"Stephen, Mr. Stanton, whatever. I went to the game with him and that was it," she said.

He stopped the questions as he peered at the television, and jumped at the converter on the coffee table to turn up the volume.

The local sportscaster had started showing game clips of the Blades win, and showed a good closeup of him during a Burysport time-out. He smiled and liked the look of that green suit on him.

The smile vanished when the local broadcaster moved to the next clip. What came next caught his attention. He noticed it caught Catharine's attention, too. The sportscaster relayed the news that Dutch had signed a free agent contract with Leinster.

He glanced quickly at Catharine.

"Glad you had a good time at the game tonight with Stephen, or excuse me, with Mr. Stanton," he said sharply. "I'll be in my office. Don't bother me."

"Now why would I bother you, Douglas?" she snapped. "Good luck figuring this out."

He waved his hand at her and went to his office. He eyed the picture of him being carried off the ice and Dutch in the background.

He clenched his fists.

"I'll be getting even with you, Dutch Felvin," he sneered. "Fuck you, Dutch Felvin."

CHAPTER 33

It hadn't taken Dutch long to accept the request of the Monarchs.

After Sonny had made the trek to Ship Cove he jumped at the chance to play again. He had the money from his contract buyout from the Blades. He was a free agent without compensation, and he acted as his own negotiator with the Monarchs. It didn't take long to strike a deal.

While Sonny yammered in the background with Mr. and Mrs. Felvin about what he'd been doing with his life, Dutch had called the Leinster general manager and discussed salary.

He didn't ask for the moon.

He knew better.

The Monarchs were giving him an opportunity to play the game he loved once again. With less than three months or so to play in the regular season, he only wanted a little to get by.

His original contract bonus from when he was drafted into the NAHA remained in a bank account in Ship Cove. Through the years he had saved enough money to build that dream house of his on the lake.

The Monarchs were a small budget team, but he agreed on some numbers. He made sure he asked for some incentive bonuses if the Monarchs got past the first round of the playoffs.

A deal was struck within one hour. When the conversation was done, he slammed down the phone and screamed at the top of his lungs.

"I'm a Leinster Monarch," he shouted. "Damn."

Dutch's move to Leinster was the talk of Burysport.

Douglas was pissed off that Dutch re-surfaced, but he wasn't surprised. His plan to ruin Dutch had almost come to fruition. He hadn't really counted on the Sonny Rufus connection, but it had happened.

Right now, he had to put thoughts of Dutch aside. He had his Blades in first place and was worried about the club peaking too soon.

Burysport started off the second half of the season against the Monarchs, and he fumed when the Monarchs didn't dress Dutch in either game.

The first game was in Burysport, which also marked the return of Sonny. He bristled behind the bench when Sonny received a nice hand from the full house and bit his lip when the fans booed at the mention that Dutch had been scratched from the game.

The Blades won four to one, but the game was not without incident. He put out one of his rugged young players late in the game and lined him up beside Sonny with a face-off deep in the Leinster zone. He had sent the youngster over the boards to tangle with Sonny.

He watched his tough guy grab Sonny by the left shoulder and nail him with a solid right hand to the face, but his smile quickly disappeared as Sonny grabbed the Blades' winger, flipped him to the ice and threw half a dozen punches.

That was not what he wanted.

He then watched Sonny skate toward the Burysport bench, restrained by a linesman.

"You're a fucking pussy, MacLeod," Sonny yelled. "You want to see me fall, better send someone tougher than that. Why don't you try and take a piece of me?"

He ignored Sonny's challenge.

"We'll see you again tomorrow night, Rufus, you stiff," he said. "Tomorrow night keep your head up."

The next night, he scowled when Dutch was scratched again. Even a three to two win didn't satisfy him. He tried again to get Sonny into a fight, but it didn't happen.

Pacing the hall after the game, he waited for his players to get on the bus so they could travel home.

He was alone in the bowels of the arena when he saw the familiar figure walking the other way.

He couldn't resist.

"Hey, Felvin," he bellowed. "How's it feel to be in Leinster, loser? Played your cards right, maybe you'd be on a real team and not with this cartoon organization."

He watched Dutch continue to walk.

"Can't say anything, huh, Felvin?" he continued. "Nothing, huh? Doesn't surprise me. My back's not to you. Yeah, sure, keep walking, coward. Keep walking. We'll see each other again."

With that, he watched Dutch disappear into a doorway.

"Pussy," he seethed. "He's scared to death."

CHAPTER 34

Conrad was on top of the world.

He had to go to the bathroom for a whiz after he read the story about the Blades already on the verge of clinching first place. When he emerged from the bathroom, he just about pissed himself when his brother Stephen and three of his pencil-pushing cronies were seated around his desk.

This had never happened before.

He thought for sure Stephen was in Baltimore for the week to oversee a project. Instead, here he was with three men he had never seen before.

He fumbled for words.

"Um, hey, ah, uh, um," he mumbled.

"Conrad, take a seat. We need to talk," Stephen said.

Conrad hit his left knee on the corner of the desk as he approached his chair.

"Fuck," he yelped.

He noticed the others raise their eyebrows and he took a seat and immediately reached for some paper clips.

"Um, uh, so big brother, what brings you all here? Boy, the Blades are sure doing well, huh? That what this is about?"

He eyed Stephen, who passed him a file as thick as a big city phone book.

He started to sweat when Stephen asked the others to leave the room.

"Conrad," Stephen began. "Dad would not be happy."

"Huh?" he croaked.

"Conrad, I gave you the responsibility of running this hockey team because it was something I thought perhaps you could handle," Stephen said. "Perhaps I was wrong."

Finally, Conrad found some nerve.

"I don't know how you can say that, Stephen. The team's in first place. We're getting good crowds. We've got a great coach, who, I should add, I hired in the first place," he crowed. "Things couldn't be better. The Stanton name is getting good results."

"Conrad, your spending is out of control and that is something you were warned about," Stephen said. "Your bills are outrageous. You go on the road and rent four or five adult movies. All your bar bills are charged to the company and you don't look after anything. You have showed no signs of fiscal restraint. You are so far over your personal budget, you could never pay it back. And the season's not even over, Conrad. We get calls from hotels saying you're not paying bills, and you don't do anything to justify these expenditures. That is something Dad wouldn't stand for. To tell you the truth, it is something I will not stand for."

Conrad was dry in the throat, but he raised his voice.

"Well, well, well, I'm the goddamn general manager of this team. I mean I'm the owner. I run a hockey team, something you know nothing about, Stephen," he raged. "You think you're just like Dad. He hated me. You hated me growing up. Now I have to listen to you tell me how to run my business when you know nothing about it. This is a team you didn't want anyway and now that I'm making it a success, you can't stand it. You sit there all prim and proper and you can't stand the fact I'm doing something successful. I told myself I'd run this company one day and show you and the old man that I am capable of doing whatever it is I want to do."

He was cut off.

"Conrad, you haven't done one thing to help this hockey team," Stephen said. "How you hired Douglas MacLeod is beyond me, but you've had five people quit this year in the team's office. We've had so many complaints about the way you treat people, that we've lost count. You are irresponsible. I'm afraid I'm going to have to make a change and you won't like it."

Conrad heard the word "change," and snapped.

"Change, huh, Stephen?" he fumed. You're not going to get the best of me. The old man tried and he couldn't and neither will you. Go fuck yourself. Take your goddamn money problems and shove them up your ass. I hate you just like I hated Dad. You can't do anything to me. I'm a Stanton."

He threw the stack of papers Stephen had presented to him to the floor and watched as Stephen reached into his breast pocket.

"What the hell's that, bigshot?" he sniffed.

"It's Dad's will, Conrad," Stephen replied. "It says, in part, 'Stephen Stanton shall be in sole charge of the Stanton Group from the day of my death. Stephen Stanton shall control all interests in the company. My youngest son, Conrad, shall receive a monthly sum of monies to be determined by Stephen Stanton.'

"That's all you need to know, Conrad. I came here to tell you all the bills have been paid. I came here to tell you I was going to keep you on, just maybe put a bit of a leash on you. That's changed after your little tantrum.

"Conrad, you're fired."

CHAPTER 35

"I can't figure it out, something's up," Dutch said as he opened his hotel door for Sonny to enter.

He wasn't going to bother with an apartment in Leinster, but had turned down Sonny's offer to shack up with him through the end of the season. The Leinster Plaza would do just fine.

"Yeah, something's up, Dutchie boy. You know me too well to get around that," Sonny said.

Life had been good for Dutch since he reunited with Sonny in Leinster. Even though he hadn't played for the Monarchs yet, there was excitement in the dressing room.

Leinster had played tough against the Blades, and even their two losses still left them in third place in their division. Only a complete collapse would leave them out of the playoffs. With his arrival down the stretch, he knew the team had added offensive support, and more importantly, leadership.

He would make his Leinster debut at home on Friday night, and the game was already a sellout.

He practiced hard with the Monarchs. The old muscles awoke to his demand, even though he had told his new linemates he would quick-shift early.

Now, though, two days before the game, he was going out for supper with Sonny, who told him he had a surprise waiting.

"Hang on a second, Dutchie boy," Sonny said. "I forgot something in the car."

Seconds later he returned.

Dutch hadn't moved. He was still sprawled out on the bed when he came to attention and got up quickly.

"Dutchie boy, I'd like ya to meet Alexis. Alexis, meet Dutchie boy," Sonny said proudly.

Dutch smiled and shook hands with Alexis.

"I've heard a lot about you," she said.

"Well, that's funny because I haven't heard a thing about you," he replied and grinned.

With that, the three laughed and sat down.

"Alexis, you must be some sort of angel to settle this thing down," Dutch said with a nod toward Sonny.

"An angel or crazy," she replied.

"Well, let's celebrate," Sonny whooped. "I got the two people I love the most with me right here, right now, and Dutchie boy, it looks like you're second on that list."

Dutch shook his head and collected his jacket.

"Will wonders never cease?" he said. "Yep, let's eat and you two can fill me in on everything. Something tells me we're going to need a long night."

CHAPTER 36

This is odd, Douglas thought, as he read the FAX.

His Blades were a couple of hours away from the start of a three-game road trip and he had just received a request from Stephen Stanton. It said he wanted to meet Douglas at noon hour at the Stanton Building.

He realized things were starting to unravel. He needed to talk to someone, but there wasn't anyone who would listen anymore.

He regretted tearing up the dressing room after a win earlier in the month. Despite the victory, he went ballistic because he didn't like the team's power play.

He had lost all contact in his home life.

He attempted to talk to his wife one night, but ended up leaving the house and sleeping in his office.

"Catharine, I need to talk to you," he had said. "The players don't seem to be listening. It's as if I'm walking a tightrope with them. They don't seem to understand what it takes to win. You need commitment."

He didn't like her reply.

"You shouldn't be talking about commitment, Douglas," she said. "That's the one word in life you know nothing about. Of course your team won't listen. You traded one of the most popular players in the league and suspended Dutch. You never smile. You're always pissed off at the world. This world doesn't owe you a favour, Douglas. You have to treat people better. That includes me. It includes our kids, too."

His anger spilled over and he blurted out what he had wanted to ask her for a month.

"So, are you screwing Stephen Stanton, or what?" he said. "Tell me right now. Are you?"

He watched her eyes widen.

"Pardon me?" she hissed. "Am I screwing Stephen Stanton? You don't talk to me anymore, you barely talk to our kids, and you ask me that question. You know what? Maybe I should start screwing Stephen Stanton or someone else. How would you like that, Douglas? What kind of question is that? You are such an insecure asshole. As much as I hate to admit it, Douglas, I'm your wife. It sickens me to say that. If you really want to know, no, I am not cheating on you. You're giving me an awful lot of reasons to do it, but I'm not. So why don't you take your pillow and get out of the house. Go sleep at the rink. It's the only place you love anyway."

"Yeah, well I've got a meeting with your boss this afternoon," he said. "You want me to tell him anything for you?"

"Get out of my face," she bit back. "Please, Douglas, leave me the hell alone."

He left the house in a rage and raced to the Stanton Group building for his meeting with Stephen.

At five minutes before noon, he was in the reception area of Stephen Stanton's office. Seconds later, Stephen emerged from the office and introduced himself.

"Hi, Douglas. Stephen Stanton," he said. "Come on in and have a seat."

Douglas settled into a leather chair.

"I must admit I'm surprised you've asked me here," he said. "Where's Conrad?"

"Mr. MacLeod, we've had a little change. Conrad is no longer a member of the Stanton Group. He has relinquished his duties with the company and with the Blades," Stephen said.

Douglas was shocked.

"I must admit I'm surprised all of this has happened," he said. "Conrad certainly put a lot into the hockey team."

"You don't have to pretend with me, Mr. MacLeod. I am fully aware you are behind the success of the Blades," Stephen said. "We both know Conrad is incapable of achieving success by himself. That may sound cold, but it's the absolute truth."

"Well, maybe somewhat, but I'm still a little surprised," he said. "I know he had his ways about him, but I thought he was doing okay. From my position anyway."

He watched Stephen re-adjust his glasses.

"Right now, you have three or four months left in the season and I feel you are qualified enough to run the ship from here on in from a hockey standpoint," Stephen said. "The Stanton Group will look after the business side of things. If you need something, please don't hesitate to ask. We will carry on and support you one hundred per cent. We realize the team is good for Burysport. The Blades are actually making money this year. I'm sure you understand that is the bottom line for this company."

"Certainly I understand," Douglas replied. "It just seems everything has happened so fast around here lately."

Stephen cleared his throat.

"Unfortunately Conrad was trying to milk money away from the profit line," Stephen continued. "Right now we want you to concentrate on making the Blades a winner and we'll make sure we concentrate on keeping the Blades a winner financially."

With that, the meeting was over.

"It was a pleasure meeting you, Douglas. We'll be wishing you luck the rest of the season. Thank you," said Stephen.

Douglas nodded goodbye, left the office and pushed the elevator button for the basement floor.

"What in the hell was that?" he murmured.

He looked at his watch and realized he had an hour before the team bus left for the airport to start the Blades' three-game road swing.

Suddenly he realized he was now in full control of the Blades.

"You are on your way now, Douglas MacLeod," he

chortled. "On your way to the big time again, baby."

CHAPTER 37

The Blades became the first team to clinch a playoff spot even though it was only the first of March. Leinster hung tough in third place. The Monarchs were hopelessly out of any chance to move up in the standings but had an eye on the playoffs.

Dutch had settled in nicely with the Monarchs, even though his first four games had him winded and pointless.

He knew it would only be a matter of time before things started to fall into place for him and he was right. He was embraced by his Leinster teammates and paid them back when he broke out of his skid in his fifth game and he scored twice, including a goal in his first shift. He also added an assist in that game and dropped the gloves for the first time as a Monarch, where he whipped some young pup.

Leinster was assured of a playoff berth. Whether it was third or fourth in the division remained the only mystery.

Sitting with Sonny, he spoke glowingly about the move to Leinster.

"I can't believe it here, Sonny," he said. "I feel like I'm twenty-five again. I honestly thought it was all over a month ago, then you show up on my doorstep. We've got a good crew here, man. I hope we make some noise. That building's loud. I don't remember it like that when we played here with the Blades. There's just great atmosphere."

"I told you, Dutchie boy," Sonny said. "As long as we're together, we can have fun anywhere. Anywhere at all. Except maybe at MacLeod's place."

He roared with laughter.

"How about him screaming at me there in the rink that night after the game?" Dutch recalled. "Calling me everything in the book. Man, I wanted to turn around so bad and go after him. It took everything I had not to say something or take him up on what he was saying. I can't believe that guy."

"You don't have to worry about him anymore," Sonny responded. "He's gone. He's done. I talked to some of the guys and they told me MacLeod's turned into a raving lunatic. So bad they fired dopey Stanton and replaced him with one of the Three Stooges."

It was all such a change from Burysport.

"You know, it surprised me how much I actually miss Burysport," Dutch said. "Maybe I took it too much for granted, I don't know. I mean, I thought we'd be lifers there, ya know? Play a few more years, but retire a Blade. Think of the times we had there. I wouldn't trade them for anything in the world."

"I know, Dutchie boy," Sonny said. "But ya gotta move on sometimes. It was great. I don't miss it that much, but I hear what you're saying. Maybe some day you can go back and visit in the summer. Who knows. Let's eat. I'm starving here."

He watched Sonny dig into his meal.

He still kept a keen eye on the progress of the Blades. He had heard about MacLeod's antics. Still, he had more important things on his mind. The playoffs on the horizon, less than a month away. He was ready for the joyride.

CHAPTER 38

Catharine was beautiful in a black skirt and white blouse covered by an attractive blazer. She was a showstopper.

Heads turned as she entered the restaurant and found her dinner companion.

Seated at the corner booth, their intense conversation was interrupted by a waiter, who scribbled their orders and scurried to the kitchen.

Having been momentarily sidelined, she took little time to get back to the brunt of the conversation.

She looked at Stephen.

"So," she said, "when the player has the puck, he has to be first over the blueline or it's an offside."

"Right," he replied. "The puck always has to cross the blueline first. Even the player with the puck can't cross first and then bring it in with him or it's offside. The puck is the key. Everyone follows the puck."

She laughed.

"Now just to confuse you even more, if a player has the puck behind his own blueline and he passes it to a teammate that's across the centre ice line, that's offside, too. That's called a two line pass. Lots of fun, huh?"

Both of them giggled.

She was surprised Stephen had suddenly taken an interest in hockey. He told her he was too busy to care about sports and never played them as a child.

"I never played a game once in my life," he said. "My days were spent in textbooks. The other kids my age all played hockey, baseball, football or whatever, but I was always around my dad. That's what I wanted as a kid. I wanted to learn about business. I wanted to be as successful as my father. I never even read the sports pages before now."

Now he was interested.

"Well, I'm glad you decided to come to a game with me," she said. "Hockey is such a great sport. Some say it's too violent, but that's part of the game. I grew up with it in my family, I guess, so it's just second nature to me."

She watched him toy with his salad.

"By the way, I met your husband for the first time earlier," he said. "He seems a whole lot different than he does when he's coaching."

She sighed.

"Douglas has seemed a whole lot different about a lot of things lately," she said. "Anyway, that's for another time. We're here to talk hockey."

"I don't know what it's been, lately, but I feel so much better," he said. "It's like I've been worrying about business all my life. Going to the games with you has shown me another side of life. My batteries seem recharged or something. I'm even reading the paper to find out what's going on with the team. I'm really glad to get out. It's something I never really did. No wonder I can never get a date!"

"I don't know about that," she said. "You have to be one of Burysport's most eligible bachelors."

"Yeah, bachelor," he said. "Mom always said I was never the type to marry. I got married way back when. Just to do it, I guess. I haven't seen my kids since the divorce. They don't even know I exist. Maybe Mom knew something I didn't."

"Well, let's go to the game tonight," she said. "The hockey seems to help both of us."

"I have to tell you, I'm looking forward to the playoffs. I understand the hockey gets even better," he said. "They say they call it the second season or something like that."

She nodded.

"A hockey player adjusts his schedule from the start of the year to the boring middle part and then for the last few weeks of the season," she explained. "When the playoffs get here, they somehow are able to turn it up to another level. I know Douglas was always a better player in the playoffs because the games meant more. Everything seemed to mean more then."

That surprised her.

For a brief second she reflected back to those days when she lived for the chance to watch Douglas play hockey.

"So, is everything all right at home? I noticed you didn't want to talk about it a few minutes ago?" he said. "If that's off base, please tell me."

The question took her aback.

"Well, he's devoted to the Blades and we don't get to see each other as much as we'd like. But we're used to it," she said. "After years of this you learn to have a June to September life."

"That has to be tough," he said. "The team's on the road so much, you probably don't get to see each other that much."

"We make do," she said. "You live and learn, I guess."

"Listen, changing the subject," he said. "I've really admired the way you've come and taken on so much at the office. It's been great to see. Just being around you seems to give me energy. You have that type of personality."

"I don't know," she said. "Getting up and going to the office has been great. I've appreciated the confidence you've shown in me. You didn't have to do that, but I'm glad you did. The projects you've had me on have been great. The challenge has been wonderful."

"I'm thinking of even more challenges for you," he replied. "That's for later. Right now, we should finish here and get to the game. I don't want to miss the warmup. I find I even like that, even though I could do without the music."

"Sure," she said, laughing. "Let's go and have some fun."

The Blades toyed with the opposition and won by five goals.

She had a huge laugh during the game when Stephen

joined the fans in the wave and she covered her eyes in mock shock.

At the end of the game, Stephen walked her to her car and asked her out for a drink.

"This may not be the right time and place, Catharine, but I have something to ask you," he said.

She looked at him uncertainly.

"Sure," she replied.

She climbed into his car and went to his house.

Stephen parked in the garage and told her to wait as he got out and opened her door.

"Why, you're such a gentleman," she mocked.

"I guess I lied to you earlier," he said. "Not all my life has been business, you know."

She walked beside him into the kitchen where he pulled out a chair for her.

"So, what is it you wanted to talk about?" she asked.

"Catharine, I haven't known you for a long time, so this may be a little quick," Stephen explained. "It's something I've been thinking about since we went to our first game, and I wanted to know if the time was ever going to be right."

"You certainly have me intrigued," she said. "Tell me, please."

"We've built our business on taking risks, Catharine," he continued. "I like to believe it's what sets us apart from other companies. Out of all the projects I've handled, this has suddenly become a big one for me. This is a special challenge and I believe, no, I know, you can do this."

"What? Please tell me," she pleaded.

"Catharine, I'd like you to become the general manager of the Burysport Blades," he blurted. "You're my choice. Douglas has the job now, but I want someone to do the job by itself. I need to know how you feel."

She was floored by the proposal.

"Well?" he asked.

She closed her eyes.

"I'll do it on one condition," she said.

"What's the condition?" he asked.
"We wait until hockey season is over," she replied.
"Done," he said quickly.
She shook his hand.

CHAPTER 39

Dutch was nervous.

He had played eleven regular season games with Leinster and had eight points, but now it was playoff time. The Monarchs were in for a huge test in the opening round against Albany and he felt the tension.

He sat naked in his hotel room, talking to Sonny who was reading a newspaper.

"Man, Albany has such a wicked powerplay. We can't be taking penalties against them, Sonny," he said. "They'll kill us."

"Yeah, whatever, Dutchie boy," Sonny said. "We've got the team. We're going to be okay. I haven't seen you this nervous in years. You're not going to puke, are ya?"

He did indeed puke, minutes before the series started, but he felt a lot better when Leinster won the first game and he had two goals.

The series switched after that and he felt his age as they went six games. The Monarchs won the sixth game at home, and he joined his teammates for the bus trip to Springfield immediately after the game to start the next series.

He sat with Sonny as the bus rumbled out of town.

"I'm not sure I'm going to make it, Sonny," he said. "I feel like I'm dead. I'm not sure I got anything left."

Sonny sat with an icepack wrapped around his rib cage.

"That prick hit me pretty good. I never saw him coming," he groaned. "Man, we're a couple of fine messes, aren't we? Least we got two days off. I'm staying in bed until the first game, I can tell ya that."

Back in Burysport, Douglas wasn't giving his team any days off. They had a longer rest after easily winning their series, but he had the Blades on the ice every day.

He scowled at Trace before going out to practice.

"What kind of crap are you writing, anyway?" he growled. "I'd like to know where you get off telling people I should give my team some time off. I don't see you coaching. You write, I'll coach. How about that."

"I just thought some of the guys could use a rest," Trace said. "No big deal."

"No big deal?" he snapped. "This is what it's all about. You have no idea of the pressure we're under here. Maybe you should sit down and figure it out. I don't give a damn what you think."

With that he stormed onto the ice to start practice. He was busy figuring out that there would be at least five NAHA coach's jobs available when the axes fell on several of them in the off-season. He felt a championship with Burysport would be his ticket to the great life of the NAHA.

He watched in glee as the Blades went out and swept their next series.

"One more series and this thing is over," he gloated to himself. "I'm on my way. Oh, yeah, on my way."

Things were not so easy for the Monarchs.

Dutch coaxed out of himself every last amount of energy and strength he had left to keep Leinster on course.

After losing the first two games to Springfield, the Monarchs valiantly fought back to tie things entering the fifth game. Springfield won the next, but he scored three times in the sixth to force a seventh and deciding game.

On the ice in Springfield before that last game, he was startled to see Douglas in the stands during the pre-game warm-up.

He glided over to Sonny in the corner.

"See who's here?" he said.

"No, what's up?" Sonny asked.

"MacLeod's here scouting the game," he replied. "Prick's down at the far corner behind the glass. Let's give him something to remember."

The teams retired to the dressing room to prepare for the game when the Leinster trainer walked over to him with a newspaper open at the sports page. He read the story outside the dressing room. He couldn't believe the quotes by Springfield defenceman Tad Knowlworth.

"We know they're a defeated hockey team," the story said. "You can see it in their eyes. They thought they had it earlier in the series, but I don't think they have anything left in the tank. Their older guys are tired and we're wearing them down. We're fresh and ready to show Burysport there are two teams in this league, not just one. Leinster has been a challenge, but we feel we're ready for the big test."

He waited until all the players had settled in before walking to the middle of the room.

"Listen up," he yelled. "Guys, we've been down. I know it, you know it, we all know it. It appears to me, Springfield knows it, too."

He read aloud the quotes in the local newspaper compliments of Knowlworth.

He grinned at the reaction the article caused, led by Sonny's string of profanity.

"Listen to me, you guys," he raved. "I joined you guys late, but I'm not ready to pack this season in yet. I've been through hell this year, and we've been through hell together. This moron said the wrong things. We owe it to everyone in this room to find something in us. I don't know where it is, but this is the grittiest team I've ever been involved with. What ya say, Sonny? You going to take this shit? What about all of us? I wish the goddamn game was ready to start now so we could beat the hell out of Knowlworth and the rest of his team."

He made his way to his seat as the room erupted.

A few minutes later the Monarchs blistered onto the ice, and he wasted little time in sending the message to Springfield. He charged into the corner and grabbed Knowlworth, ready to make him eat his words. He tore off his helmet and hammered away until finally the linesmen intervened and pried him off.

He stood over the fallen player.

"You stupid bastard," he yelped. "Thanks for the lift, dickhead. You guys are going down tonight."

The game was only twenty-four seconds old.

Leinster, despite losing him to the penalty box for seven minutes, took his lead and pounded Springfield.

After what he did, the Monarchs played possessed and marched into the final with a three to one win.

They would face the Blades in the best-of-seven championship, set to open two nights later at the Memorial Complex in Burysport.

He was going back home. Sonny was going back home.

Together again in Burysport.

Douglas had watched in disgust as Dutch pummeled his foe, and he watched Leinster ride all the momentum that was created.

He was at the game for a couple of reasons. He was sure the Blades would be playing Springfield and he wanted to watch its style of play. Even though it was the seventh game, he felt Leinster didn't have a chance.

He also had nowhere else to go.

He had been kicked out of the house when his wife told him to pack his bags after yet another fight.

He replayed the scene on the drive to Springfield.

"Douglas, I've had enough of you. This time it's it. It's over. I want you to please leave the house," she had ordered through tears.

"You know what, Catharine? I can't wait to get out of here. I'm so sick of your goddamn yanging that I can't take it anymore," he roared. "You and your almighty ways. You're spoiled fucking rotten. I'll be out of here for awhile, but I'll come back when I damn well feel like it. Tell the kids I'll see them in the morning."

"Why don't you tell them?" she spat. "You haven't talked to them in a week, though, so why would you start now?"

He grabbed his datebook and left.

"She'll miss me," he muttered.

CHAPTER 40

Burysport was in a hockey tizzy.

The Blades were back in the final for the first time in almost a decade and their old rivals from Leinster were in town to recapture the glory years.

Two favourite sons were also returning.

Dutch and Sonny were the subject of a number of barbs and jabs from their teammates on the media requests and stories the two had generated.

"Damn, I'm not sure I'm going to have enough time to play with all the media after me," Dutch said. "Maybe I should get into television or something so I can interview myself."

He listened to more howls of laughter from his teammates as the club finished practice the day of the opening game.

Leinster had survived two seven-game series and he was pissed off the majority of media said this series would probably be a Burysport sweep.

He took Sonny to lunch, back at their favourite bar in Burysport.

It didn't take long before it started.

"Ah, damn, look who's coming?" he groaned.

Sonny glanced over his shoulder.

Arriving at his side was the fat guy from last summer's golf tournament. On his arm was Ardelle.

"Dutch, you 'member Ardelle, don't ya? Shoot, I didn't think I'd see ya again. Hope ya do well, but we're going to win."

"Yeah. Hi, Ardelle. How's it going?" he grimaced.

Sonny helped him out.

"Hate to interrupt you and your friends, Dutchie boy, but we have to eat now, so if you'll excuse us, we'll let you get on your way," he said.

They watched the two walk away.

"Hey, thanks man," he said. "You to the rescue again."

"Shit, just thought of something," Sonny said. "Gotta call Alexis."

He shook his head.

"This whole world's going crazy," he mused.

CHAPTER 41

Sunday's Daily Star headline said it all.

The bold headline print on top of page one blared "Marathon Men"

It was a tremendous game.

Both teams threw caution to the wind and played firewagon hockey. There were end to end rushes, brilliant defensive plays, and clutch goaltending at both ends of the rink.

In late May, the old Memorial Complex wilted in the heat, as did the fans.

The players were left gasping for air. There had been several vicious hits, a couple of great scraps and even some shouts between Dutch and Douglas that had the crowd on its feet. He stood a foot from the Burysport bench and screamed at the Blades' head coach.

"You fucking idiot, I should have dropped you when I had the chance," he yelled. "Ask your players. They'd love to drop you too, you misfuck."

"Shut your mouth, Felvin," Douglas roared. "You piece of shit. We're not done with you yet."

He was restrained by Sonny from going into the bench, and Douglas had to be hauled back by his trainer.

The crowd roared its approval.

Leinster had forty-one shots on goal and still trailed in the dying seconds.

With Burysport ahead one to nothing and three minutes to play, Dutch skated out of the corner on a Leinster power play.

Somehow his low blast was kicked out by the Blades' goaltender. The rebound came right back to him and his second shot was somehow stopped by the goaltender's left arm.

"Damnit," he erupted. "Put the damn puck in the net."

Leinster pushed for the equalizer but couldn't connect. With twenty-one seconds left in the third period, the Monarchs forced a faceoff deep in the Burysport end and their goaltender was on the bench for a sixth attacker.

Dutch was going to take the face-off against Kevin Barrett.

During a Burysport time-out, he skated over to Sonny.

"Barrett likes to draw to his forehand," he said. "I don't think I can beat him on that side. The kid's good. I gotta hold his stick somehow and kick the puck back. Be ready for anything. We're getting a shot on goal somehow."

He heard MacLeod scream at Barrett from the bench, "Don't let Felvin beat you. Tie the bastard up."

He skated into the circle. He heard the roar of the crowd. He watched the linesmen adjust the players anticipating the drop of the puck.

He felt the sweat pour off his chin and watched it drip onto the ice. He moved into the circle and took his position for the draw.

The puck dropped and he slid his right hand on top of the Burysport center's stick, rendering it useless. He spun around and kicked the puck back to the blueline.

He watched Sonny move in two steps and let fly with a wicked slapshot.

Barrett hammered him with an elbow after his clever ploy, and he was staring at the ice when Sonny unloaded. The wails of the Burysport crowd told him his team had scored, and he jumped up and joined in the bedlam of hugs.

He looked up at the clock.

Sixteen seconds left in regulation, and overtime was coming.

A tentative first overtime period passed. Both teams had just six shots on goal.

A second overtime went by the boards. The Blades had the best chance to win on a breakaway, but the Leinster goaltender made a huge save.

By the midway point of the third overtime, the players were exhausted.

The fans were exhausted.

Sonny dug the puck out from along the boards and spotted Dutch at his own blueline.

Dutch took the pass and started a two-on-one break.

He moved into the zone and held onto the puck as long as he could. At the last possible second, he feathered a pass to his linemate. The puck flicked over the Burysport goaltender for the winning goal.

The Leinster bench exploded in a mad rush of players.

Dutch found Sonny in the chaos and they hugged tightly.

He highfived with as many teammates as he could find.

It was almost six hours since the game began.

He was exhausted.

He left the ice, and it was then he saw Catharine standing with Stephen Stanton.

He raised his right hand and stuck out his index finger.

Years ago as she stood in the stands one night in Augustine after his team had won, he had left the ice and given her the same salute.

He watched her bring her hands to her mouth.

CHAPTER 42

All the emotion that blanketed that memorable first game was nowhere in sight in the second in front of another fullhouse.

The Blades dominated.

Prior to the game, Douglas foamed into a tirade and tore a Leinster replica sweater to shreds.

"You think this team is better than us?" he cried. "They're nothing. They're lucky. Go out there and show them who the best team in this league is. Don't ever let them beat you again. This is the biggest series of your lives. Play that way."

He slammed the door on his way out and then watched Burysport win eight to four.

Back in Leinster for the third game, Douglas grimaced as Dutch scored his first goal of the series early in the first period and the Monarchs scored again two minutes later. The Blades fought back to tie, but Dutch scored again in an eventual five to two win.

Leinster now led the series two games to one.

Between games Douglas stayed holed up in his hotel room. He notified the front desk to stop calls through to him after he received four crank calls from Leinster fans.

One night he was in a foul mood as he wolfed down a room service dinner.

He tried to engineer the tactics that would get the Blades a win Friday night and send the series back to Burysport even.

He hadn't spoken to his wife in almost a week, but that was the least of his worries. That would have to wait.

He watched game film searching for Leinster's weaknesses.

He had to find a way around the Monarchs' defensive style.

And he did. He pushed all the right buttons on that wild Friday night in Leinster. He was successful on an illegal stick call, and his team scored on the powerplay, riding that to a five to one win and going back home tied at two wins apiece.

"That's better, you guys," he roared. "That's the team that was the best all season long. You stuck it to them. We're going home and we're winning. Great job. Now we have to crank it up even more. Kick these losers when they're down."

In the fifth game, Burysport started the third period fast and scored two quick goals for a four to two lead before the Monarchs raced back to tie with nine minutes left.

He was left speechless when Sonny scored his second goal of the final.

"Someone has got to pick him up on the blueline, damnit," he roared. "You jerks played with that guy. You know what he does. Keep him contained. He has no business scoring against us."

He was celebrating minutes later when the Blades scored again for a five to five tie in a wild game of adrenaline changes.

He called a time-out right after the goal with five minutes and thirty-three seconds left in the third period.

He demanded his players tighten up defensively around the Leinster forwards.

"Make them pay the price. The ref's not calling a penalty

at this stage. Make them pay," he yelled. "Don't let anyone in front of our net."

He slammed the bench door.

Right after the whistle, the Monarchs waded into the Burysport zone and worked diligently along the boards for possession. Dutch came out of the scrum with the puck and had a clear path for the goal but was hauled down from behind.

There was no call by the referee. The Blades quickly turned the puck up ice and Douglas was ecstatic when a long shot went in for a six to five lead.

He couldn't resist.

"Nice job, Felvin," he shouted. "Nice effort out there. Good work. Stay on the ice. You'll help us win this series yet. Big games still kill ya, don't they?"

He was satisfied with that outburst. He knew Leinster was stunned by the sudden turn of events, and Burysport scored an empty net goal for a seven to five win. The Blades held a three games to two series lead and sat in the driver's seat as they entered the sixth game back in Leinster.

"That was a damn penalty if I ever saw one," Dutch groaned.

He was leaning on the shower post in the visitor's dressing room.

"He hauled me down, Sonny," he said. "I don't care how much time was left in the game. Ya gotta call that, man."

"Tell me about it, Dutchie boy," Sonny replied. "I saw that, I figured we had a powerplay coming."

He let the water beat on his back.

"That fucking MacLeod," he grimaced. "Always there with a knife to stick in my back. Hear him chirping after that sixth goal, Sonny? Gotta have the last word. I haven't said dick to him since that first game. I gotta get him back."

"Don't bother with MacLeod, Dutchie," Sonny said. "Just leave him alone, okay? We got enough to worry about. I want this thing so bad. We need two wins, Dutchie boy. Let's worry about us. Screw MacLeod. Don't play his game, man. This is about us now."

"You're right, Sonny," he said. "Maybe just a punch when this is all over and we win. Okay?"

"Whatever you want, Dutchie boy" Sonny said. "We win, you get a free target."

CHAPTER 43

The movie theatre was pretty much empty.

Perfect.

Dutch and Sonny occupied two seats in the back row. Dutch had gingerly placed his worn body into the cramped chair and noticed Sonny did the same thing.

He had decided a movie was the perfect way to relax on the day before the sixth game of the AHA final.

What else were they going to do?

Neither the Monarchs or the Blades practiced on the off day, so for two hours and fourteen minutes, he and Sonny never said a word but watched a mystery unfold on the big screen.

When the movie ended, they remained seated to read the credits before they turned to each other.

"Whatdya think?" Dutch asked.

"Awful," Sonny replied.

"Two thumbs down. Let's roll," he replied.

He winced as he got up a little too quickly.

The two left the theatre and milled around the mall. They shook a few hands and received words of encouragement from fans in different stores.

Neither minded the aimless stroll through the air conditioned mall. The sun outside was relentless and made the late May day feel like mid-summer.

They left the mall and jumped into the truck Sonny leased from a local car dealership.

Sonny steered the truck down to the Leinster waterfront and they climbed out and walked toward the boat dock, which was still pretty much empty this early in the season.

Dutch dipped his feet in the still cool water.

"Never thought I'd be here," he said. "It's been a hell of a wild crazy ride."

"Who would've thought, huh?" Sonny replied.

Sonny leaned against a concrete block.

"What's going to happen to us, Dutch?" he asked. "You and me been together an awful long time. We're getting to the end, aren't we? Could be the last game for us both tomorrow. Ever think of what's going to happen?"

Dutch stared at his reflection in the water.

"I had a lot of time to think when I was out, but I still don't know what's up," he answered. "I can still play a few more years. You can still play a few more years. Hell, I won't be back here. I doubt it, anyway. You'll be here. You've found your place. You got Alexis. Me, I'm not so sure."

He leaned back.

"You know, sitting out showed me I ain't ready to hang 'em up yet. I'll be thirty-five this summer. Thirty-five, Sonny, can you believe that? I remember just starting out playing and one guy was thirty-five when I broke in. Damn. Thirty-five to me at the time seemed ancient. You know what I mean?

"Now I'm here and I see the kids coming in. Sometimes they give me incentive, you know? I see them looking at me. I see them looking at you. They're thinking the same thing me and you used to think about the old guys. I know they're saying no way when I'm that old will I still be playing. Before you know it, it's here. Comes a time when you have to think about what you want to do when you grow up, but I'm not ready. I know I'm not ready. I can still play and I will still play. Where? Who in hell knows?"

"Well," Sonny said, "if you don't think you're down, think you can help win us one more game?"

He looked at Sonny's weathered face.

"I'll see what I can do about that, my friend," he responded. "We're going to find out, aren't we?"

With that, he took his feet out of the water and slipped

them into his loafers. It was time to leave.
　　"I'm not done yet, Sonny."

CHAPTER 44

The national anthem was lost after the first bar.

Dutch could barely hear himself think. The crowd in Leinster was fever pitched.

The noise quickened the pulse of the players, the coaching staffs, and the training staffs, and it didn't take long for the place to raise its noise level.

He tipped a shot from the blueline into the top corner early in the first period for a one to nothing lead.

He listened to the public address announcer as he took a seat on the bench.

"Leinster goal, scored by number sixteen, Dutch Felvin."

Pandemonium.

He liked the way the announcer carried out his last name.

He knew it was still early and there was a lot of hockey to be played, and he watched across the ice as Douglas attempted to get his players back into the game. There was rarely a chance when he didn't sneak a glance at Douglas behind the Blades' bench. He wanted the victory so bad he could taste it. A win in this series would be his ultimate revenge.

And Leinster held on to the early lead. He sank his ninth goal of the playoffs into an empty net with eight seconds left to seal a wildly dramatic two to nothing Leinster victory.

He was named the game's first star.

As he skated out the fans chanted "One more win, one more win."

He embraced Sonny in the locker room.

"Have ya got one more in ya, Dutchie boy?" Sonny bellowed.

"We'll know in forty-eight hours, Sonny," he said loudly. "I think we've both got one more in us. MacLeod's dying over there now, buddy."

His long, long troubled season, many highs, many lows, many changes, personality conflicts, drinking binges, everything, had come down to one game.

He wanted to be by himself.

"I have to win," he said. "I've gotta help us do this."

CHAPTER 45

Fans pressed their noses to the plexiglass as the teams warmed up for the seventh game in Burysport.

Dutch stood at centre ice. He was surrounded by a number of pucks and picked them out to pass to his teammates.

The players, each and every one of them from Leinster and Burysport, skated with extra zip as the clock over centre counted down the time left in the warm-up.

Finished with his chore, Dutch quietly joined his teammates in line rushes for two-on-ones and three-on-twos.

He scanned the stands and saw Catharine flanked by Stephen Stanton and her two kids.

"Hey, Sonny," he said. "I see Catharine's here again with the big wheel Stanton. What's that all about?"

"Cripes, Dutchie boy. You got more than that to worry about right now," Sonny said. "Get it together. Let's go."

Biding his time in warm-up lines, he glanced at the stands for familiar faces. There was his favourite bartender. The fat golfer was there. Ardelle was there, too.

He shook his head as memories came flying back.

This used to be his rink. This used to be his crowd. He owned this town. Now he was at the other end of the ice. He was wearing different colours. All because of Douglas. He needed the satisfaction of revenge.

The age-old siren wailed to snap him out of his fog.

He sat at his locker with a towel draped over his head. He heard the coach enter the room with a "Listen up, guys."

He peered out from under the towel.

"Guys, this has been a great ride," the coach said. "What a great run. What a great season. Not one person predicted we'd be here when the season started. One win away from winning the whole goddamn thing. Imagine that? I'm so proud of you guys. You work hard for everything. You're all winners. Now we just have to go out and prove it. Stay away from the dumb penalties. Don't let the emotion get the better of you. Stay within yourself. Do your job. Felvin, you start."

He walked to the middle of the room when the coach left. He said three simple words as the siren screeched for the teams to hit the ice.

"Kick ass, boys," he shouted.

The players erupted from their stony silence, and he listened to them shout and watched them slap each other on the shinpads.

They were greeted with lusty boos and jeers. He was the last one on the ice and only heard the small contingent of Leinster fans who made the trip.

The noise he heard next shook him.

The arena exploded as the Blades hit the ice.

It was game time.

Game seven.

CHAPTER 46

For all the hype and hoopla, the game was off to a slow start.

"It's okay, guys," he yelped from the bench. "Keep it simple out there. Don't miss our assignments. No mistakes. No mistakes."

He missed a great scoring opportunity midway through the first, and he closed his eyes in agony when Sonny fired a shot over top of an open net.

The second period started lightning quick and the Monarchs rang a shot off the post twenty seconds in. But the Blades collected the puck and raced up ice with it.

Dutch watched the play from the bench, and there was nothing he could do as a Burysport player fired a quick shot. He breathed again when the Leinster goaltender stopped it.

He turned to his coach.

"Holy fuck, is it ever loud in here," he yelled. "Can't hear myself think."

After that big save, the teams lined up for the face-off deep in the Monarchs' zone. On the bench, he jumped to his feet and screamed at his teammates to watch a winger who had snuck away.

It was too late.

The Blades' forward got the puck and drilled a snapshot past the goaltender's stick side. Burysport was ahead one to nothing.

"Fuck!" he screamed. "C'mon guys. Pick that idiot up

out there. Stick to your man. C'mon. Don't let that happen.
Let's get it back right now."

He steamed on the bench.

He peered across the ice and saw Douglas slapping the
backs of his players.

He glanced further into the stands and saw Catharine
and Stephen in a celebration embrace.

"What in fuck is that all about?" he muttered.

The clock ticked down to forty-four seconds to play in the
second period, and the Monarchs had the Blades hemmed into
their own zone. A wild scramble ensued off a Sonny snapshot,
and the rebound bounced into the high slot.

Sonny's defence partner bolted toward the loose puck
only to have a Burysport player poke it past him into open ice
for a breakaway.

A forehand deke. A shift to the backhand. And another
Burysport goal.

The red goal light triggered another tremendous
celebration for the two to nothing Blades' lead.

Thirty-five seconds left in the second period.

He immediately went over to Sonny's partner.

"It's okay, kid," he shouted. "Don't worry about it.
We're coming back here. It'll be all right. We're going to
regroup. We need you strong here."

The period ended.

The Blades left the ice to all kinds of noise. Dutch's team
was twenty minutes away from losing it all.

He heard the familiar rally cries. Dig down. Let's pick it
up. C'mon boys, we're not down yet. They echoed through the
Leinster dressing room.

He sat beside Sonny.

"Hey partner," he whispered. "We need a goal before the
five minute mark or we're screwed. We need something. Keep it
going back there. Something's going to go in. These pricks can't
shut us out, baby."

He knew the Blades would break the final period into
four segments. Kill the first five, then the second five, the third

five and the final five minutes.

He didn't get his wish. His Monarchs still trailed by two goals with just over fourteen minutes to play.

He felt it slipping away.

At the ten-minute mark his eyes sparkled thanks to Burysport getting caught with too many men on the ice for a minor penalty. It was next, he gambled.

He darted for the bench and told his coach to call for a stick measurement on Kevin Barrett. He knew Barrett used a big curve on his stick. If he was successful, the Monarchs would have a five-on-three power play. If he was wrong, Leinster would be penalized for delay of game and the teams would play four players aside.

It was a ploy he had waited for.

When the referee offered the stick to the penalty box area, the Monarchs' bench erupted.

He had made the right decision. It was a two minute penalty to Burysport for illegal equipment.

Leinster capitalized.

The Monarchs gained Burysport's zone and took their time. There was a lot of room to move with a two-man advantage.

Sonny got the puck at the blueline and slid a pass toward the corner. Suddenly, the puck hit a Leinster skate and caromed into the Blades' goal.

Dutch was behind the net when the puck went in and he rushed to his teammates, pumping his fists.

"Yeah," he shrieked. "Great job, Sonny boy. Shoot the puck. Put it toward the net. Anything can happen. C'mon guys. We're moving now."

Leinster had shaved the lead to a goal and still had another power play to work with. That was the bonus of a goal before the first minor penalty had expired.

But the Blades killed off the minor and the teams returned to five players aside for the final eight-and-a-half minutes of regulation play.

Leinster repeatedly tried to get into Burysport's zone, but

the Blades' defence held strong.

On the bench, Dutch watched the time on the scoreboard tick down to seven minutes.

He got the tap on the shoulder to go out for a face-off in his own zone.

He skated to the bottom of the face-off circle.

He took his mouthpiece out to speak to Sonny.

"Sonny, it's time to gamble," he said. "If I win this draw to you, bank it high off the glass. Their guy hasn't been tying me up. I'll go right through their defencemen. Make it work. Don't screw this up, Sonny. Just like we worked on for years. Make it happen."

He sensed fear in Sonny's eyes. If the plan didn't work, the Blades' defence could knock down the pass and get a shot on goal.

It was a huge risk.

He won the draw clean and he was right. His opposing centerman never laid a stick on him as he bolted to daylight. Sonny did as he was told and clanked the puck off the glass along the boards and out where he collected it in fullstride.

He was one-on-one with a Burysport defenceman.

He cut straight into the middle of the ice. He thought for a brief second he couldn't beat the Blades' defenceman to the outside.

"He's got me out there," he thought. "Gotta move the other way and shoot."

He made a little shift at the top of the face-off circle and let fly a snapshot, using the defenceman as a screen. The goaltender didn't expect the shot from that far out and it beat him low to the stick side.

There were six minutes and fifty-two seconds to play and his goal created a two-two tie.

He watched Sonny skate furiously to join in on the mob that surrounded him. They had combined one more time.

"What'd I tell ya, Sonny?" he screamed. "I told you man. You knew you had to have faith in me."

"Damnit, Dutchie boy," Sonny roared. "I was scared to

death, man. Don't ever do that again."

Skating back to the bench, he looked over at the Blades and smirked as Douglas flung a water bottle the length of the bench.

"Take that, dickhead," he yelled across the ice.

The clock continued to count down.

Now was the time not to make a mistake.

With fifty-three seconds to play, the Monarchs moved swiftly into the Burysport zone.

Dutch had been playing the last few minutes, but he didn't feel fatigue. He carried the puck deep into Burysport territory. The Blades tightened and the crowd shifted to the edge of their seats.

The Burysport goaltender made a nice save off his wristshot from a bad angle, but the puck moved to the blueline.

Sonny's partner collected the loose puck and moved in on goal. He fired up the cannon slapshot he possessed and unloaded.

Out of nowhere, a Burysport player slid into the play and blocked the shot with his shinpads. The puck bounced all the way back toward the Leinster goal.

There it was. He could see it. But he was stuck in a maze of players in the opposition zone. There was nothing he could do except watch as Burysport's Barrett flew toward it.

The clock reached the forty second mark.

He soared back to get into the play, but it was too late. He could only watch as the Leinster goaltender gambled and left the crease in pursuit of the loose puck.

He could hear the Burysport player's skates cutting into the ice as he chased him.

He heard the crowd gasp.

And he stared in disbelief as Barrett got to the puck first. Just ahead of the Leinster goaltender.

Barrett grabbed the puck and went wide of the sprawled keeper.

With an empty net to shoot at.

"No. Fuck, no!" he yelled.

CHAPTER 47

In an unusual move the Blades fired Douglas even though they won the championship. The fans were shocked initially until Trace broke a story that detailed his vendetta against Dutch and his selfish mannerisms toward his players.

"The past came back to haunt MacLeod more than he ever wanted it to," wrote Trace. "Everything Felvin stood for, whether it was his lifestyle or his friends - which included Sonny Rufus - stood in MacLeod's way of happiness. He couldn't bear to coach the player he viewed as the one who ended his career. It was a shameful way to act and spoiled what would have been the best season ever, not simply a great season."

Douglas was outraged when Catharine was named general manager. He was livid when she fired him.

He stormed into the Stanton offices and demanded a meeting. He ignored the secretary's plea not to go into Stephen's office, instead bursting through the door.

"I saw the two of you together," he screamed. "Do you think I'm stupid? What kind of joke is this? You're with my wife right in front of me and then you hire her as general manager. A woman can't survive in this game. You're crazier than she is."

"Mr. MacLeod, I'm afraid I'm going to have to ask you to please leave. Immediately," Stephen said. "You have no right to be here. If this continues, I'll be forced to call the police."

"Go ahead and call the fucking police," he roared. "Call them right now. I hope this whole thing blows up in your face. You're as stupid as your fucking brother. I'm going away, Stanton. I'll be gone. But I'll be watching. Don't think I won't be watching. You'll be sorry for all this. I'm a winner."

He stormed out of the building.

Down the stairs, he entered the parking garage and climbed into his car.

He wiped tears away from his face. He had to get away. He was losing his emotional grip. He had lost his wife. His kids. His job.

He pointed the car north. Toward Augustine.

He had to get out of town.

CHAPTER 48

Four days later the sun pelted down as Dutch eased his weary body onto a sandy beach. He was far, far away from home on the beautiful San Diego shoreline.

He was alone. That's just the way he wanted it.

But he closed his eyes and the painful memory came flooding back. It hurt him more than any injury he had ever suffered. The sun and surf of San Diego did nothing to ease that pain.

He replayed the final play over and over. He re-lived the scene where Barrett got to the loose puck first. He had watched helplessly as he skated to the edge of the crease for an easy tap-in goal into an empty net to give the Blades the AHA championship.

It had been too much.

He had slumped to the ice and buried his head as the Blades celebrated. He had watched fans climb over the boards to join their team. He had watched as Douglas stood atop the bench, pumping his fists.

He had stayed on the ice for the traditional handshake at the end of the series.

He had even taken Barrett aside.

"You're a good kid," he said. "You're a nice hockey player who's got a career ahead of him. Don't get lazy. Keep playing hard."

He refused to shake Douglas's hand.

As he went through the line of Blades, he heard Douglas scream at him, "Go home and retire now, Felvin. You're all done now. I'll send you a bottle of champagne for your troubles. Loser."

He shook his head. For once it didn't seem to matter.

He left the ice and didn't look back.

He spoke briefly with Sonny in the somber dressing room.

"I'm so sorry, Sonny," he consoled. "I thought we had it when I scored. We had a great ride, buddy. A great ride."

Sonny reached out and shook his hand.

"You're the best, Dutchie boy," he sobbed. "I love ya."

"Listen, Sonny," he explained. "I'm getting outta here as soon as I can. I'm going to get me some San Diego weather for a week or so. When I get there, I'll let you know where I'm staying. Don't let anyone know where I'm going, okay? I need some time."

He was on a plane to San Diego eleven hours after the heartbreak.

He had crossed the border into Tijuana the first night and got drunk, firing back tequila and beer, and staggered back to San Diego to pass out on the beach, just out of reach of his seaside hotel.

When he awoke, he climbed into his hotel room for a shower.

An hour later, he was back on the beach.

It had been an hellacious season.

What had started with so much promise had crashed because of the feud with Douglas. It all seemed so far away now. He had found a new lease on life in Leinster, but he knew he was a hired gun. He understood the Monarchs wouldn't be interested in signing him for another season.

It was nine-thirty in the morning when he dug into a huge cooler and hauled out his third beer.

"Ah, another frosty," he murmured. "How drunk are we going to get today, fellas?"

He drank deeply from the third beer and reached to

rummage a smoke out of a dented package. He brought it to his mouth. He lit the cigarette and drew on it heavily.

The booze and the cigarettes seemed to help somehow as he took another swill and threw his head back. He closed his eyes. He saw the goal again.

The sound of ice rattling in his cooler brought him back to reality.

He opened his eyes.

In front of him stood Catharine.

What the hell was this?

He whisked off his sunglasses and tried to avoid the beer he had spilled.

He squinted through the sun.

He tried to find her eyes.

"Boy, don't you look great," she commented. "Is there a problem? Every time you see me, you're knocking over drinks."

He still hadn't said a word. He finally stood up and took a haul off his smoke before he tossed it to the sand and exhaled.

"Um, excuse me," he said.

"Yes?" she replied.

"No, ah, excuse me. You'll have to excuse me for being a little, no a lot, surprised to see you here," he said. "Don't tell me Douglas is here to join me for a beer?"

She burst into laughter.

"Dutch, please put your sunglasses on or you're going to bleed all over yourself with those eyes," she answered. "I know it sounds strange, coming all this way, but we need to talk."

"Talk? Again?" he said. "I gotta tell you, there's a lot more I'd rather be doing with you than talking. We haven't talked too well together in a long time. By the way, how in hell did you know I was here?

"Certain friend of yours," she replied.

"I'm going to have to have a little word with old Sonny when I get back. If I get back, I guess," he said. "Well, anyway, again. You came all this way to ask me something. Something that couldn't have waited, huh?"

"To tell you the truth, I'm here as kind of a messenger for

Stephen Stanton," she started.

"Hey, wait. What the hell is that all about, anyway?" he asked. "Every game in Burysport, I see you with him. You guys an item? That must have driven your husband nuts."

"We're just friends, Dutch," she said. "A lot more than that was driving Douglas nuts. I had to ask him to leave the house, Dutch. It was all becoming too crazy. Mom is down looking after the kids now. I haven't heard from him since the Blades won. Oh, sorry. Didn't mean to mention that."

"Yeah, nice cheapshot," he said. "Thanks for reminding me."

"Well, since you've been here playing the beach bum role, you probably haven't heard a thing," she said.

"Heard what?" he responded.

"Stephen hired me as the general manager of the Blades," she said.

He nearly choked on his drink.

"He hired you as what?" he yelled. "General manager? You gotta be kidding. That's amazing. Hey, congratulations, I guess. You gotta be the first woman general manager in pro hockey. You always did know the game."

He shook his head some more.

"How about this, huh? It gets better," she said. "I don't know where Douglas is, but I fired him two days after the parade in Burysport. Fired him and kicked him out of the house within three weeks. That's bad for anyone's ego."

Dutch brought his left hand to his forehead and wiped his face.

"Am I still dreaming here, or what?" he wondered. "Damn. You've given me information overload. Just seeing you blew me away. Now this. Maybe I should have read a newspaper. Wow!"

"Dutch, Douglas and I are through. We have been for a long time," she said. "What I did at the professional level has nothing to do with my relationship with Douglas. I spoke with a lot of the players and they all said they don't want to play for him ever again, championship or not.

"He blew it at home, too, Dutch. He lost his position as a husband and more importantly, as a father. We couldn't do it anymore."

He stared at her.

"Hey, I know I'll look like the supreme bitch when word gets out we're separated and I've fired him, but life's a bitch. The papers will have a field day with this one."

He rubbed his eyes.

"That's all pretty amazing stuff, but you didn't have to come all this way to tell me about what's going on in your life," he said. "Don't get me wrong. I love seeing you, but this could have probably waited. It's not like we talk every day."

Catharine cleared her throat.

"That's not what this is about right now, Dutch," she replied. "I'll get to the point. This is business. You don't have to answer right away, but I'm going to ask you something. I have to return to Burysport, but I'd like to have an answer in a week at the most, assuming you're not planning to stay drunk that long," she said.

"An answer? About what?" he asked.

When their conversation was over, he was stunned. He barely heard her tell him she had to get back to the airport for the noon hour flight home. He was floored when she asked him. He was stunned when she traced the scar at the bottom of his chin and brought her finger up to his lips. He didn't kiss her back when she brushed her lips against his.

He watched her walk away.

He reached into the cooler and pulled out his fourth beer.

He lit another cigarette and watched the surf. It roared in like a lion only to splash harmlessly against the shoreline.

"Well I'll be damned," he said.

He took a huge swallow of beer.

"Well I'll be damned."

He took a long, hard drag off the cigarette.

Suddenly, he stood up, threw down his cigarette, and dashed toward Catharine who had reached the parking lot.

"Hey!" he shouted. "Hang on a second."

He walked over and stood beside her as she reached into her purse and fumbled for the keys of her rental car.

"How do you feel about missing your plane?" he suggested. "Business can wait."

Hours later, she sat with her legs crossed over his on the hotel room sofa.

He was stripped to the waist.

He peered into her eyes.

"You know, you're my boss now," he said.

"Well, that means you better do a good job, huh?" she replied.

"Maybe I should get started right now," he whispered.

"I think you should," she said.

He kissed her.

She left the light on.

CHAPTER 49

Everyone at the Burysport Golf and Country Club was decked out in shorts and tee-shirts, embroidered with the charity golf tournament logo.

Sonny sat at a table near the back with Alexis, a diamond ring shining on her finger.

Sonny had proposed to Alexis a couple of days after the loss. He even got down on one knee. They planned to marry after the next hockey season.

All was well for Sonny. He had a fiancee and a new two-year contract to play out his career with the Burysport Blades. Catharine knew how popular Sonny was in the community and she wanted to bring him back.

His return was welcomed in Burysport after the fans learned of the story behind his trade.

Above the din, there was an announcement from the front of the room.

Trace introduced himself.

"Many of you probably know me better as a reporter for the Daily Star. But I'm happy to announce I've traded in my pen and am now the director of communications and media for your AHA champion Burysport Blades," he said.

The crowd broke into applause.

Trace introduced a number of the players who had remained in Burysport to soak up all the adulation a championship team receives.

He then introduced Stephen and Catharine.

"Today we're here to enjoy a great day of golf and to raise money for a great cause," Trace said.

"We're also here to introduce the new head coach of your Blades."

People gasped in anticipation. They craned their necks in order to get a look at who would stride to the podium.

Sonny bowed his head in his hands. A huge smile adorned his face.

Seconds later, Trace made the announcement.

The new head coach arrived at the podium to a thunderous ovation.

"I believe ya all know me," he said. "It's nice to be home. By the way, I'm also going to play another year."

He said it with a huge smile.

Dutch was back.

#######################################